A MISSION FOR THE CZAR

Gorg Huff
&
Paula Goodlett

Gorg Huff & Paula Goodlett
Visit us at www.Warspell.com

Printed in the United States of America

First Printing: June 2021
1632, Inc.

eBook ISBN-13 978-1-953034-89-2
Trade Paperback ISBN-13 978-1-953034-90-8

CONTENTS

For Kevin Evans, the real Vadim. 1632's steam head and an all around maker of things. Including an actual working AK rifle.

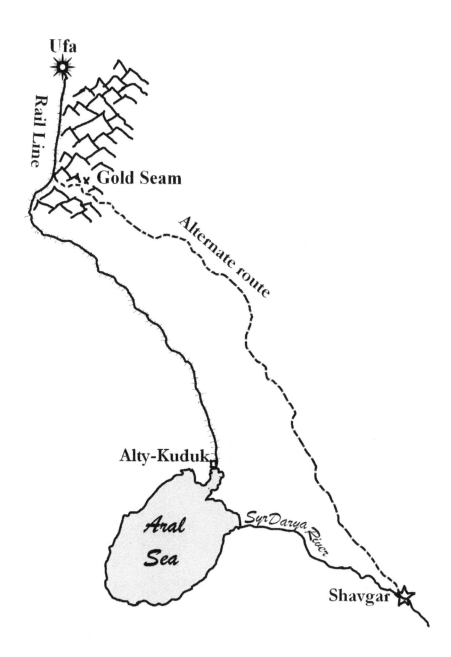

A MISSION FOR THE CZAR

CHAPTER 1: A MISSION FOR VASILII

Location: Ufa
Date: June 1, 1637

Vasilii Lyapunov fiddled with the mechanical pencil in the breast pocket of his tunic. It was a nervous habit and Vasilii had reason to be nervous. He was waiting for an audience with Czar Mikhail. Vasilii was not used to audiences with the czar, and would prefer to be even less used to them than he was. He was, at his core, an engineer. He built stuff. He didn't really do politics if he could avoid it.

At least that was Vasilii's image of himself.

The reality was more complicated.

"The czar will see you now," said the young man who was guarding the door.

Vasilii, dressed in his best but still nervous, went through the door. He didn't think he'd done anything wrong, but he couldn't think of any other reason for the czar to want to see him.

✳ ✳ ✳

The door opened and Vasilii heard Czar Mikhail say, "Come in, Vasilii."

Vasilii went in and saw the czar lounging in a well-padded chair that had more in common with the La-Z-Boy than a throne. Next to the czar's throne was a comfortable loveseat, in which resided Bernie Zeppi and Princess Natalia Gorchakov, by now commonly known as Natasha.

Bernie was the czar's up-timer advisor, while Natasha was the czar's advisor on matters technological, because she had been running the Dacha since it was founded at her family's dacha in 1632 and had been running the Ufa Dacha since it was established on their arrival in Ufa, not quite a year ago.

Across from Bernie and Natasha on a couch, sat Colonel Ivan Smirnov. He and Vasilii had met several times and Vasilii did not like him much. Smirnov was a high-ranking member of a family at the upper end of the lower nobility. He was arrogant, opinionated, self-centered, with a sense of entitlement, and undeniably good at his job, which was surveying.

After Vasilii bowed, Czar Mikhail waved him to the couch that Smirnov was sitting on.

Vasilii sat as far away from Smirnov as the couch allowed.

"Now that we're all here," Czar Mikhail said, "Jangir Khan is entranced by the notion of a railroad and wishes to begin the process of building one as soon as possible."

Well, Vasilii thought, *that explains why Smirnov is here, but what the fuck am I doing here?*

"Why, Your Majesty? The Kazakh are a . . ." Smirnov paused in the manner of someone looking for a polite way of describing something offensive. ". . . migratory people. Why not simply carry the goods from China in their caravans?"

"Surprisingly enough, Ivan," Czar Mikhail said, "caravans wandering along their own route across the plains are quite difficult to tax. But a railroad is located just where you put it. Jangir Khan is hoping that the advantage of the ease of travel provided by the rail line will make up for the taxes he plans on charging on goods transported from China to here and vice versa."

Vasilii looked around at the czar, at Bernie, at Natasha, still wondering what he was doing here. Bernie was grinning and Natasha had a little half smile like she knew a secret, but then Natasha usually had a little half smile like she knew a secret. And she usually did.

Vasilii was tempted to ask what he was doing here but restrained himself.

Smirnov didn't. "If you wanted someone to consult on the steam locomotive," he said, "Vadim Ivanovich would've been a better choice." Then he looked over at Vasilii and added insincerely, "No offense intended."

Bernie snorted and everyone looked at him.

Then Czar Mikhail sighed, and spoke directly to Vasilii. "The reasons you're here instead of Vadim Ivanovich are first that you are rather more diplomatic than Vadim and, second, that you outrank Colonel Smirnov here."

Vasilii was shocked by the coldness in the czar's voice. He looked over at Smirnov and saw the man's face getting red. He tried to pour a little oil on the troubled waters. "Colonel Smirnov is a colonel of cavalry. I have no military rank."

"That is quite true," the czar said. "However, I am appointing you as the leader of the delegation, which will give you a civilian rank equivalent to a brigadier general." He looked at Smirnov and sighed again. "Colonel, you are an excellent surveyor and mapmaker and a first rate soldier, but you give offense as easily and as quickly as you take it. For right now, Jangir Khan is the most powerful noble in my realm. Soon we're going to have to deal with Sheremetev's armies to the northwest. I don't need to be dealing with a war to my southeast at the same time."

"Your Majesty, I'm an engineer!" Vasilii whined.

"You were also the delegate from the Dacha to the Constitutional Convention. And you served well in that posting, don't deny it, Vasilii. I was there," Czar Mikhail said, and then added in a mutter, "And got the Dacha special privileges they really shouldn't have gotten."

Vasilii didn't agree with that. He believed that graduating from the Dacha with a bachelor's or master's degree should be the *mestnichestvo,* social equivalent, of rank in the lower nobility. It wasn't like they got lands with the title, after all. Which didn't matter at the moment, because it was clear there was no way he was getting out of this. "What is our mission, Your Majesty?"

"Didn't I make that clear? Colonel Smirnov will be surveying and mapping the route for a rail line from Ufa to Shavgar, the capital of the new state of Kazak. Or a rail line from here to where the Syr Darya Jaxartes enters the Aral Sea. Which would be considerably shorter, but would then require steamboats along the Syr Darya.

"Meanwhile, Vasilii, you will be negotiating with Sultan Togym about the structure of the rail line. Who will own what and how much of the revenue will go to Jangir Khan and how much will go to the crown."

"But I'm an engineer!" Vasilii complained again. It did no good. While, in theory, Vasilii was there to talk about steam engines, in fact he was to be the czar's negotiator for the railroad, determining who would pay for what and who would take what profit.

"The other thing Colonel Smirnov will be doing is finding good line of sight locations for a radio telegraph system that we want put in place," Czar Mikhail said. "I have Jangir's approval for that much now, though we weren't planning on doing it until we got more tubes. But if we're going to be building a rail line, radio links become more urgent."

"We still don't have that many tubes," Bernie said.

"I know. We'll send a tube unit with the mission. When you find a likely spot—" He looked at Smirnov. "—give Vasilii the coordinates and he'll send them back to us, and we'll send out a team to set up a station. This isn't exactly a secret, but don't make a big deal out of it." The czar grimaced. "I'm supposed to be waiting until

I have Kazakh's trained to operate the stations in the Kazakh lands. Ahh!" He grinned. "The State of Kazakh."

The meeting went on and eventually Czar Mikhail called it to a close. Then, just as they were leaving, he said, "Vasilii, wait a moment."

Vasilii got a resentful look from Ivan, who didn't like anyone getting the czar's attention when he wasn't.

Once Vasilii was seated again on the couch, Czar Mikhail said, "Once you reach Jangir Khan, I want you to impress on him that he needs to actually start having people vote if he wants to have representatives in congress. And see if you can get him to do a state constitution."

That, of course, led to more complaints that he was just an engineer. Which didn't impress the czar any more now than they had before, and Vasilii got a lecture on internal Kazakh politics. While in theory an autocrat like Mikhail, in fact Salqam-Jangir Khan's situation was closer to the situation of Russia before Ivan the Terrible. The clan leaders were essentially kings in their own right, with a loose allegiance to the khan. A lot of them weren't going to be all that happy with the new statehood of the Kazakh lands and Vasilii was to encourage Salqam-Jangir Khan to use as much honey and as little vinegar as he could manage with them.

"More carrot and less stick, Vasilii," Czar Mikhail finished. "Make that clear."

Location: Ufa Dacha, Room 22B
Date: June 1, 1637

Vasilii opened the door to their apartment to see Miroslava lying on the bed naked, with her nose in a book. Intent on not being distracted by her state of undress, Vasilii asked, "What are you reading?"

"Basic Russian dictionary," Miroslava said. The basic Russian dictionary was a picture book, in that it showed the printed word next to a picture of the item. In spite of that, it wasn't designed primarily for children, but for adults just learning to read. And Miroslava had already read it through. By now Vasilii knew that Miroslava had an eidetic memory, but he also knew she took a certain comfort in rereading books that she had already memorized. He didn't understand why. It was just the way she was.

She rolled onto her side, so she was facing him and asked, "What did Czar Mikhail want?"

Vasilii grimaced. "He's sending me on a mission into the Kazakh Khanate. We're going to have to come up with a route for the China railroad."

Miroslava lifted an eyebrow, but all she said was, "When are we leaving?"

"You're not going!"

"Why not? And who's we?"

"It's dangerous!"

Miroslava waited, and Vasilii realized she asked two questions and was waiting for the answer to the second.

"Colonel Ivan Smirnov will be in charge of mapping the route and in command of a unit of streltzi who will act as guards. I have to go along because Smirnov is an ass."

Miroslava gave a jerky little nod which caused certain parts of her anatomy to jiggle in a most distracting manner. Then said, "How is it more dangerous for me than for you?"

"You're a woman!" Vasilii said before he'd really thought things through, then hastily added. "A beautiful woman. I, at least, am unlikely to be the object of an attempted rape."

"I am more likely to face attempted rape here without you, instead of there with you."

There was at least some truth in that, Vasilii knew. Miroslava's new status gave her some protection, but her old status as a bar girl, and her beauty, both turned her into a target. As long as Vasilii was here in the same city with her, simply his existence provided quite a bit of protection. But how much of that protection would continue after he was gone from the city was hard to say. On the other hand, how much his protection would be worth out in the hinterland, surrounded by Kazakh warriors was another question he didn't have the answer to. "You've never even ridden a horse."

"And I shouldn't be riding one now," Miroslava said. "If we're scouting routes for a railroad we should take a train engine."

Actually. Vasilii thought, *that's not a bad idea.* They didn't exactly have a train engine as in a locomotive engine. What they did have was a couple of steam tractors. The steam tractors weren't as powerful as a locomotive engine would be, but they wouldn't be pulling nearly the load either. And using one of them along the proposed rail road route would act as a decent test bed to determine whether or not the ground would support the weight of a train. "I don't know what we would use for a wagon though."

"You should go take care of that, then." Miroslava sat up, which caused more jiggling, but the enticement that had been there in her earlier movements was missing now. "I have things to do if we are going to be spending time in the Kazakh plains. When are we supposed to leave?"

Vasilii realized that he had lost the argument about whether Miroslava was going or staying. And he didn't really regret the loss. He was glad that Miroslava preferred to be with him.

* * *

After discussing things with Miroslava he went to see Vadim Ivanovich.

Vadim, as usual, was in the steam engine factory.

The steam engine factory had a poured concrete floor. It wasn't the only building in Ufa with a concrete floor either. By now there were many small cement factories dotted around the various tributaries of the Volga River. It had become a cottage industry. And as the capital of the United Sovereign States of Russia, Ufa could afford to have the cement shipped in.

There were any number of one-off steam engines scattered around the factory floor in the process of being built, rebuilt or taken apart for parts. There were smaller shops around the large factory floor, but Vadim was in one corner of the main room, lying on a shop creeper pulled halfway under a steam boiler, using a large monkey wrench to pull a flow valve.

Vasilii, recognizing the always greasy shop coveralls Vadim wore, walked over to the corner calling Vadim's name. Vadim ignored him.

He kicked Vadim's foot. "Come out of there, you illiterate peasant."

Vadim rolled out from under the boiler, looked up at Vasilii, and grinned.

"What for, you effete bookworm?" Vadim reached up with a greasy hand. Vasilii took it and hauled the man to his feet. Not an easy task, as Vadim weighed two hundred and fifty pounds if he weighed an ounce.

In fact, Vadim Ivanovich was a streltzi craftsman who had been only semi-literate when he arrived at the Dacha, and while Vasilii had a better theoretical understanding of steam engines, Vadim had a feel for the things. They almost talked to him. Over the last four years, Vasilii had learned to trust Vadim's "feel" for steam engines, and they had become friends, mostly within the limits that their different stations allowed, but not entirely. Bernie's influence was stronger in the Dacha than anywhere else in Russia. It was so strong that Vadim Ivanovich, at least on the shop floor, felt comfortable teasing Vasilii about his education.

"So what brings you to a place where men actually work?" Vadim Ivanovich asked as he wiped his hands with a dirty rag.

Vasilii hooked a thumb at a door. "Come into the office and I'll tell you about it."

Seated in the office with a couple of small beers, Vasilii and Vadim talked about railroad trains and the engines that pulled them. All steam engines have certain things in common, but there is a great deal of variation.

In Vasilii's mind the many variations were divided into three general categories:

First were: Crude steam engines; in which water was pulled directly from the river, fed into the boiler, run through the engine, and allowed to escape as steam. Doing it this way was simplest and easiest to build, but used more fuel, and the boilers inevitably developed problems with rust from the corrosive elements in the water that was boiled. Most of the people who died in steam engine accidents were using this sort of steam engine.

Second were: Industrial steam engines which were well-built and had evaporators so that the water used by the steam engine would be pure, and had condensers so that it could be recirculated and lose less of the energy produced by the external combustion. They were really built in only two places in Russia, right here in Ufa and in Murom, the city formerly owned by the Gorchakov family.

Then there were: Delicate steam engines. These were the ones where weight and efficiency were at a premium. These were steam engines that went in the dirigibles and would go in the multi-engine steam aircraft that Vasilii was working on.

While Vasilii worked on the delicate steam engines, Vadim Ivanovich worked on the industrial steam engines, which were no longer experimental, though they weren't that far from it.

Vadim Ivanovich set his small beer down and said, "Okay, Vasilii, what's this all about?"

Vasilii sighed and looked around the office. It was a smallish room, about ten by fifteen. On one wall was a set of open wooden cubby holes containing pieces of paper which Vasilii knew from experience would be plans and notes on projects in the works. There was a drafting table in one corner and a somewhat larger table that they were seated at. There was also an ice box in another corner, from which they'd gotten their small beers. Having put it off as long as he could, Vasilii looked at Vadim and explained what the czar wanted.

"You can't. I have too much to do! I can't be running off with a bunch of horse barbarians."

Vasilii grinned. "I'm actually not here for that, but it's an excellent idea." Then he sighed and went on, "Or at least it would be, if the czar hadn't already decided to stick me with it. I'm actually here to consult with you about what steam engines are available so that I'll have a better idea of what they can pull up what sort of grades."

"We're talking about the single rail tracks, aren't we?"

"Probably, but that hasn't been decided yet," Vasilii agreed. "Heck, it hasn't really been decided whether to go directly to the Kazakh capital city or just head for the Aral Sea. That's going to depend on the terrain, which is why Colonel Ivan Smirnov is going."

"Thank heaven it's not me!"

"You may not be thanking heaven in a moment, my friend," Vasilii said. "I want one of your tractors."

"Not going to happen," Vadim said. "The army needs those to build the roads and fortifications around Ufa."

That was true enough. Ufa was suffering under a chronic labor shortage in spite of the number of serfs who had come to Ufa since Czar Mikhail's emancipation proclamation. On the other hand, the czar had made it perfectly clear that this trip was of the highest priority. "I'm afraid the city walls are going to have to be made by grunt labor until you can get another steam tractor built."

Vadim was not happy, and Vasilii understood why, but there wasn't really anything he could do about it. Vadim was so unhappy that he insisted on confirmation from the czar, which arrived the next day.

Meanwhile, Vasilii had other people to see.

Location: Ufa Dacha Radio Center
Date: June 4, 1637

Viktor Bogdonovich Fyodorov wasn't any happier than Vadim had been, and he had a telephone that had a direct line to the czar's office in the Kremlin. For this, he used it, and he wasn't thrilled with the results, but they were straight from the czar. So Viktor stopped arguing and got to work helping.

"How's your fist?"

It took Vasilii a moment, but he remembered. "I don't have one. At least not what an actual telegraph operator would recognize. Besides, the radio system in Russia uses teletype machines and paper tape. I remember from the Happy Bottom murders."

"Darn it, Vasilii, those are expensive and you're going to need a tape reader and repeater at every station along the route."

Vasilii pointed at the phone and Viktor grimaced. "But even so, you want someone along with a good fist in case the machines break down and you need to send something in Morse. And I really *don't* have anyone."

Location: Ufa Kremlin
Date: June 5, 1637

Bey Nazar sat again in the same small room that he and Sultan Togym had used when they negotiated the end of hostilities. It was the same room, appointed in very much the same way, but everything else was different. Now Nazar wasn't just a Kazakh noble, but a noble in the USSR as well. And he was here after three days of hard riding and changing horses to emphasize how important the new railroad was to Salqam-Jangir Khan. He looked around the room. Bernie Zeppi was there, along with a colonel and the expedition leader, neither of whom Nazar had met.

"I rode ahead with some of my men to let you know that we're going to be bringing some of the wagons of our people. The khan wants the surveying team to be comfortable."

"Wagons" wasn't the word he used. The word he used, *khibitkha*, was a Kazakh term that referred to a yurt on a large wagon, pulled by up to thirty-six oxen.

Half an auyl, one of the traveling villages that followed the herds, was coming to Ufa to provide traveling accommodations to the surveying party.

There was a snort, and Nazar looked over at the overdressed Russian colonel.

The expedition leader, whose name was Vasilii Lyapunov said, "Please excuse Colonel Smirnov. He's unfamiliar with your *khibitkha*. For that matter, so am I, except for reading about them, and that only this week. Is it true that they take large teams of oxen to pull them?"

"Yes, quite true. Our people follow the herds and that makes it necessary to carry our goods and our homes along with us."

"Why, that's excellent." Lyapunov smiled. "We are planning to bring one of our new steam tractors to test its suitability and to confirm that the route chosen for the railroad will support the weight of heavy trains. We believe that it should be powerful enough to pull one of your *khibitkha*. This will be an excellent test of our equipment."

"I would be pleased to see this 'trac tor' of yours." Nazar stumbled a little over the unfamiliar word.

✳ ✳ ✳

Half an hour later, in a field outside Ufa, Nazar got his first look at a steam tractor. It was big. Very big. It had four wheels, two large iron wheels in the back, and two smaller wheels in the front. It was operated by a crew of two, an engineer and a fireman. At the moment, it was pulling a large bladed contraption behind it, which had a crew of men on handles, keeping the angle of the blade right to take only a few inches of soil off the top. But the blade was twenty feet long, and even a half inch of soil was a lot of dirt in only a few feet of travel. The blade was angled, so that the dirt was piled in a continuous mound along the left side of the path that the scraper made.

Watching it work, Nazar thought that it probably would pull a *khibitkha*. If they were strung together, it might even pull two.

Location: Field Outside Ufa
Date: June 7, 1637

Vasilii Lyapunov and Miroslava Holmes walked around the *khibitkha* that was to be their home for the next little while. Vasilii found himself impressed and more than a little horrified.

It wasn't crude, that clearly wasn't the right word. For it was obvious that great care had been taken at every phase of construction. The heavy wooden floor was smoothed by the extensive use of grinding stones. The round heavy woolen tent was almost more house than tent. Its walls were thick and extensively embroidered.

Care and even artistry had been used extensively in the making of the traveling yurt. But while the same care had been lavished on the wheels, they were solid wooden wheels, not spoked. And it was quite clear that the makers had never heard of roller bearings or ball bearings. Instead, there were iron bearings. Huge iron bearings, heavily greased with animal fat.

The top of the yurt didn't have the thin steel chimney of a Franklin stove. Instead, there was a simple hole in the center of the tent roof to let out the smoke of a fire.

In other words, it was a fortune in labor, but in severe need of an upgrade. Given what the sucker must weigh, Vasilii wasn't' at all sure that the tractor would pull it.

* * *

Miroslava was more sanguine about the wheeled yurt. She noticed what Vasilii had seen beneath the artistry and the lack of up-timer influence, but she was not particularly impressed or disappointed. The world was what the world was. Besides, a Franklin stove could be installed readily enough. So could lighter wheels with ball bearings. And it was certainly big enough. The distance between the two back wheels was close to forty feet. The front wheels weren't quite so far apart, about twenty-five feet.

If changes had to be made, changes could be made.

"What do you think?" asked Bey Nazar, pride clear in his voice. Perhaps a bit of belligerence as well. As though he was expecting the "civilized" Russians to disparage his peoples' work.

Vasilii, being much more politically astute than he liked to admit, picked up on both the pride and the belligerence. "It's an impressive piece of work, Bey Nazar." He hesitated.

Bey Nazar, who had grown up in the khan's court, was as politically astute as you could ask for. He heard the hesitation and his expression showed it. "What is wrong with it?" he demanded.

"Nothing's wrong with it," Vasilii insisted quickly.

"Of course things are wrong with it," Miroslava said. "If things weren't wrong with that, then the up-timers would've landed in the

Khanate six years ago, and the kazakhs would have no use for us. That's why the khan joined the USSR, because we have things of value to his people."

Which was a generous interpretation of the khan's complex of political, military, and economic reasons for joining the United Sovereign States of Russia.

* * *

Bey Nazar looked over at the Russian woman. She was very beautiful and was wearing the new style of makeup that the up-timers and now the czarina was making popular in Russia. Kazakh women mostly didn't wear make-up, at least not while the herds were being moved, which happened twice a year. Or now, because they were here to pick up the Russians. But he hadn't expected her to talk. Not a bar girl made into a faux lady to satisfy a horny engineer. In Nazar's mind, the word engineer meant essentially the same thing as wizard. Someone with great and arcane power to whom you granted special privileges, but who lacked true understanding. He looked back at the engineer. "So what is wrong with it?" he asked again. But with, perhaps, a little less belligerence in his tone.

The engineer smiled. "I say again, nothing is 'wrong' with it. But there are things that we might be able to do to improve it, because of the knowledge that the up-timers brought."

"What things?"

"New wheels that are as strong as yours, but lighter. And axles that turn with less friction. Turn more easily."

The wheels on the *khibitkha* were as tall as a tall man and two feet wide, three at the axle. It took three strong men to lift one, and ropes and pulleys to put one on the axle. "Very well. Let's go see these wheels of yours."

"We don't have them right now. We'll have to make them. Well, we have to design them, then have to make them."

"And how long will that take?"

"I'm not sure. Maybe a week, maybe more."

"You want us to wait here a week while you design and build a new set of wheels that may or may not improve the speed of a *khibitkha*? I'm sorry, but there simply isn't time. We are supposed to meet Sultan Togym in only three weeks."

"We can work on the design while we are traveling, and give them to your craftsmen. Will that be all right?"

Bey Nazar shrugged his indifference. "Certainly."

There were three of the massive *khibitkha* in the caravan as well as half a dozen smaller wagons. "In the meantime, there is a test I would like to perform. We have a steam tractor that we were planning on taking with us on the survey trip. I would like to see if it is strong enough to pull a *khibitkha*."

Bey Nazar laughed and waved. "Be my guest." He turned to his retinue and spoke in his own language. They all had a good laugh.

❋ ❋ ❋

It took fifteen minutes to get the steam tractor into position and another ten to get it hooked up to the rigging used by the oxen to pull the *khibitkha*. All the while, Bey Nazar and his friends were displaying their amusement.

Then Vasilii waved to Vadim, and Vadim opened the steam valve. The tractor moved, the ropes tightened, and then the *khibitkha* moved.

The laughter stopped. There were a few religious gestures. And Vasilii took the opportunity to smile benignly in his turn.

After that, they spent the rest of the day packing the stuff they were taking into the *khibitkha*, and meeting the servant woman who would be looking after them. She was a slave of Nazar's household and spoke only a little Russian. Her parents, at least her mother, had been a serf that ran with her family and was later captured by the Kazakhs.

And with their introduction to Rayana, they got their first look at how pervasive the changes Salqam-Jangir Khan was instituting were. For Rayana wanted to know about voting. Women and slaves were to be allowed to vote, and no one owned their vote but them. "What is a vote? Is it like a soul? Is it a thing or an act that the khan is giving us?" she asked in hesitant Russian after they were situated in the *khibitkha*.

It was warm in the *khibitkha*, even a bit too warm. It was June, after all.

Location: South South East of Ufa
Date: June 11, 1637

They were coming out of the forest now. The area right around Ufa was all old growth forest in hill country. It was also pretty well surveyed, but four days out of Ufa the land was flattening out a bit. More than a bit, really. You could still see the mountains in the distance and the sunrise over the mountains was especially striking this morning, full of reds and oranges and blue gray higher in the sky. Vasilii and Miroslava were sitting on the wooden area that almost had to be called the front porch of the *khibitkha* as it sat still.

Not because the rest of the caravan wasn't ready to go. It was sitting still because the packing on cylinder two of the steam tractor had blown out. Again. When it was running, the tractor could pull the *khibitkha* at almost twenty-five miles an hour, which was dangerous because the *khibitkha* wasn't designed to travel at more than ten miles an hour and really preferred speeds in the two to four miles an hour range.

That was especially true since the land they were traveling over was covered in grass as high as, well, not an elephant's eye, but certainly Miroslava's. That grass effectively hid any gopher holes or rocks. That wouldn't be an issue on a rail line with a rail taking most of the weight and a graded surface for the other wheel to travel on.

But, here and now, it was a problem.

The tractor crew had banished Vasilii to the porch or he'd be helping them. By this time Vasilii wasn't a bad jake-leg mechanic. But he wasn't part of the team and he hadn't spent the last six months working on the steam tractor.

Miroslava was quietly amused at the way Vasilii's eyes kept turning from the sunrise to the tractor and the two men working on it.

He wasn't the only one watching. Two of Bey Nazar's armsmen were sitting their horses watching the work. Most of the rest were

21

milling around as the rest of the caravan rolled slowly south, still visible in the distance.

Nazar himself rode up then. He pulled his horse up next to the porch. "How long?" He pointed at the tractor.

"I don't know," Vasilii said. "The crew has banished me."

Nazar gave him a look.

"Do you stand around instructing a midwife in how to deliver a baby or a sword maker in how to make a sword?" Vasilii asked. "Those men are specialists and they know that machine like the backs of their hands. My theoretical understanding is greater, but not my practical knowledge of the machine."

Which, Miroslava noted silently, was pretty much what the tractor mechanics had told Vasilii, with considerably less profanity than the mechanics had used.

"We need to hurry. Sultan Togym will be in Druzhba by now."

Miroslava looked at the bey out of the corner of her eye. She was still uncomfortable looking at people directly. It was just too intimate. But what was changing was that she was starting to trust her interpretation of what people said and the way they said it. A bar girl needs to be able to do that, but only in a very restricted situation. It was unlikely that the client wanted to talk about artistic trends in Moscow. Or if he did, he didn't want her opinion on the subject.

What she'd learned over the past couple of months was that her way of seeing the world could be expanded to areas outside the bar.

Bey Nazar was lying, or at least not telling the whole truth.

"We have to wait for the surveying crews anyway," Vasilii said, and Miroslava noticed an almost grimace on the bey's face. It could be simply because of the delay, but it could be something more.

Gorg Huff & Paula Goodlette

CHAPTER 2: GOLD IN THEM THAR HILLS

Location: Mountain Stream
Date: June 18, 1637

Colonel Ivan Smirnov inhaled deeply of the fresh mountain air. He was standing atop a rise next to a mountain stream and had just finished tagging the place to three known locations, so he knew its location as well as if he'd had Global Positioning Satellites in the sky.

Colonel Smirnov didn't read much. Not because he couldn't, but because he was wealthy and preferred to have things read to him. He knew about GPS because he'd had articles on it and how it worked read to him. He'd also had pretty much everything the up-timers knew about map making and geology read to him. And he understood them. He was, as he would quickly tell you, an extremely intelligent man who didn't suffer fools gladly.

That was why he was so happy this morning. He was out here by himself. Even his assistants were at least a hundred yards away, holding measuring rods. He waved to them that he'd gotten the measurement and started putting his transit away. Once it was in its case, he leapt lightly down to the stream and knelt to take a drink of the cool spring water. As he was lifting a hand full of water to his lips, he saw a glint in the bottom of the stream.

He reached down and picked up the small piece of gold. He weighed it in his hand. It was at least three ounces, perhaps more. And this was gold, not iron pyrite. Ivan knew the difference.

He looked at the position of the sun and checked his pocket watch. It was early yet, only 10:30, but he decided it was time for lunch. He climbed back up to the rise and, using hand signals, told his crew they should break for lunch. Over the next hour, while eating a ham and cheese on black bread sandwich, he scouted the creek and found a seam of gold-bearing quartz in a rock face about ten yards upstream.

He had a good memory, as did most people who are semi-literate, but for this he made notes in his notebook. He wanted to be sure.

Then he climbed on his horse and rode to join his surveying crew. They were all skilled and all knew their place. They also knew that Ivan often chose to eat his lunch alone, preferring his company to the ramblings of servants. So no one asked him what he'd been doing.

Location: Camp
Date: June 18, 1637

Colonel Ivan Smirnov sat in his wagon that evening, carefully adding the notes from his surveyor teams to the map. Normally, he would resent the cramped quarters of what amounted to a gypsy wagon, but tonight he was much too concerned with other matters to pay the wagon any attention.

Having added the notes to the map, his next step would be to examine the map and design the route of the railroad based on a number of factors. Those factors would include such things as grade, soil depth, soil saturation, the location of rivers, rock outcrops, even forest density. They would *not* include how far the railroad would be from a potential gold mine.

However, in this case, the one thing he knew about the potential gold mine other than its location, was that it did not belong to him. Nor was he in any position to claim the land. It belonged to a Kazakh tribe and would remain theirs unless the railroad went within a half a mile of it. If the railroad did go within a half a mile of it, the tribe would get some stock and the railroad would get the land.

And the gold mine on that land.

The amount of stock in the railroad that the tribe would get would be exactly the same as it would get for prairie with nothing more valuable than cow dung on it. There would be no negotiations, no debate, and most definitely no option not to sell. Neither the czar nor the khan wanted to be held up by a greedy noble who suddenly discovered that a chunk of worthless cow pasture was a highly valuable right of way for the railroad.

Ivan grinned as he thought about the effect of the sudden announcement that "just by chance" the right of way of the new railroad included a gold mine. It wouldn't happen until the land was the railroad's property and the tribe had already been paid. But in a few months the stock would go through the roof as people speculated about what else might be in the right of way.

He didn't notice the servant woman who was quietly sitting in a corner cleaning and polishing his boots. In that, at least, this night was no different than any other.

* * *

Medina watched the Russian mapmaker as she did every night, but this night was different. He was excited about something, she could tell. Usually, he complained as he worked. The fire in the stove was too hot. The breeze from the windows was too chill. The food wasn't up to Ufa standards, much less Moscow standards. The wagon was too cramped to do proper work in.

Tonight, though, he didn't complain at all. He seemed very happy about something. Finally, close to midnight, he got up from the work table, took off his tunic, and went to bed. By that time Medina was snoozing in her corner of the wagon. His movements woke her, and after he went to bed, she brushed down his tunic and checked its pockets. That's when she found the gold nuggets.

Medina didn't know that there was such a thing as iron pyrite. She'd never heard of fool's gold. But her ignorance in this case was as good as Ivan's knowledge. *This was gold.* And the Russian was excited about it. Medina was tempted to take it, but she knew that she would be the suspect, so she put it back in his pocket.

She also put his notebook back in his pocket after reading his notes. Well, reading what she could of his notes. She wasn't a good reader, but she'd memorized the Arabic numbers, and she could read those.

Also, by now, she knew what coordinates were.

Location: Camp East of Druzhba
Date: June 20, 1637

Ivan Smirnov looked around. The radio set in the *khibitkha* was located next to the left wall as you faced the front where the steam tractor hooked. Near the middle of the space was a "Franklin" stove that wasn't needed this time of year except for cooking in rainy weather. Across from the radio set were the pile of sheep skins that Vasilii and his whore used for their entertainments. There was another stack of skins where the servant Bey Nazar provided slept. Assuming she didn't join in their entertainments. Ivan snorted in superior disgust.

He looked back at the radio set. There were a set of lead acid batteries next to it, carefully capped and vented. There was also a typewriter with a paper tape machine attached. Every time you hit a key on the typewriter, it punched a pattern of holes in a paper tape. At the same time it printed the letter above the holes, so that you could check to see if you made a mistake. When the message was typed, the paper tape was removed from the typewriter and fed into a roller that ran it through a reader at a set speed. It was slow by Grantville or even Magdeburg data transmission speeds, but massively faster than the fastest Morse code operator.

Contented that he knew how to operate the thing, Ivan sat on the wooden chair in front of the typewriter and began to type out his message.

It was a slow process and Ivan hit several wrong keys and each time had to repeat the whole message. But he got it all written and then fed it into the radio.

To: Kirill Amosov
From: Colonel Ivan Smirnov

At opening bell tomorrow morning you will start selling my holdings and buying stock in the Russia Kazakh Railroad company. Do it slowly Kirill without attracting attention.
Message ends.

Ivan got the confirmation of receipt from the operator at the next station.

Ivan didn't know then or ever that the radio man at the next station had read the message and spread the word. It was a tip on the market over the next few days, and raised the value of RKRC stock by twenty percent.

Location: Coordinates in Ivan's Notebook
Date: June 21, 1637

The rider found the coordinates. Not easily. He wasn't used to the new maps that the Russians used. But he found them. Then he started looking. What could Colonel Smirnov have found here that was so important?

It took the rest of the afternoon, but eventually he saw a glint of gold.

He would have matters of import to report.

Location: Druzhba
Date: June 22, 1637

Sultan Togym watched the caravan arrive with mixed emotions. He understood his young cousin's reasons for joining the USSR, but sovereign in name or not, the khan was giving up the khanate's ultimate sovereignty. It would now be a state in the USSR. And while the devil's bargain that the khan had made might well have been the best deal for the khan, it wasn't—in Togym's opinion—the best deal for the khanate.

He saw the Russian soldiers riding in formation two by two with their rifles in scabbards attached to their saddles. There were only ten of them, but those rifles made them much more formidable. The bullets from those guns would punch right through armor.

Yes, they had the threat of the czar's armies, and even more, the czar's factories to threaten the Zunghar Khanate with. But the price was too high. And this railroad that the czar and the khan were engaged in was an example of why. The khan wouldn't have been able to just seize land from the tribes, not without the support of the czar. And the czar couldn't have done it as a foreign power. Every noble in the khanate was weaker under the federal government than they were under the khanate government. And most of them knew it.

He looked down at his saddle and the AK 4.7 carbine that was holstered there. It was a powerful weapon, but it spelled the death of cavalry as a striking force. The Russians and their up-timer knowledge were like djinn, giving miracles, but twisting them so they do more damage than good.

He sighed and rode out to meet them.

* * *

Miroslava looked around. This yurt wasn't mobile. It was also at least twice as large as the one they rode in on their way here. There was a feast laid out and dancers, acrobats, jugglers, and musicians.

And, unsurprisingly, Ivan Smirnov was making an ass of himself. Questioning if any of the Kazakh nobles should be admitted to the House of Lords. Even Sultan Togym, who was the khan's elder cousin. Much less Bey Nazar, who was "just the son of a tribal leader that the khan took a liking to."

The lieutenant and the sergeant of the streltzi were looking embarrassed and Vasilii was trying to rein him in, but Smirnov had rather more to drink than was strictly good for him. The Kazakhs wore their Islam fairly lightly. They drank fermented mare's milk and other alcoholic beverages on occasion.

And, knowing that the Russians would be coming, they had brought baijiu from China. And Smirnov had developed an immediate fondness for it.

As Miroslava watched the reactions of the various Kazakh nobles, entertainers and servants, she was forced to conclude that Smirnov might actually be useful to the mission. He was certainly attracting the animus of all the Kazakh nobles to himself and Vasilii's attempts to rein him in were making Vasilii and, through him the czar, seem more respectful of Kazakh rights and sensibilities.

"That's it!" Vasilii not quite shouted. "Colonel Smirnov, you will return to your wagon and stay there until you are sober. That is an *order!*"

Colonel Ivan Smirnov turned to face Vasilii and started to swell up.

"Do *not* speak, Colonel! I have greater *mestnichestvo*, greater military rank, and am the head of this expedition. If you wish to make any of this into an affair of honor, we will discuss the matter after we have returned to Ufa and *after* I have made a full report to the czar."

Colonel Smirnov didn't back down, not exactly. Instead he came to a parody of attention, saluted poorly, did an about-face without quite falling down, and marched unsteadily out of the yurt.

How much of his sloppiness was drunkenness, how much was disrespect, and how much was simply the fact that military formalities had changed a great deal in the last few years was hard to tell. Certainly all three played a part.

After Colonel Smirnov had left, Vasilii turned to Sultan Togym. "I'm sorry about that, Highness. I don't know anyone who actually likes Ivan Smirnov, but he is very good at his job. Both his jobs. Aside from being an excellent surveyor, he is a skilled and innovative military commander. All I can truly suggest is that we use his skills and put up with his boorishness."

Location: Druzhba
Date: June 23, 1637

Sultan Togym hid his smile as a very under the weather Colonel Ivan Smirnov came into the room. It was a well lit space, the lighting provided by Coleman-style lamps. Outside was a summer storm, not common, but far from unheard of. It would be gone by midafternoon, but in the meantime the yurt was closed, and Ivan Smirnov wasn't just hung over. He was also wet.

Muttering darkly to the amusement of every Kazakh in the yurt, he used a wool felt towel to dry himself and the map case before opening it.

The case was a tube about three inches across and two feet long, made of hardened tanned leather with a leather cap, and it contained hand drawn maps.

Pulling the maps from the case and putting them on the folding table, Ivan said, "The direct route to Shavgar is turning out best after all. The Aral Sea route has some potential problems that it would be better to avoid."

"What problems?" asked Vasilii Lyapunov.

"Issues with the water table," Smirnov said a bit too dismissively, and Togym became suspicious. From his expression, Vasilii wasn't convinced either.

But Smirnov was sorting through the maps. He selected one and spread it out, using the case to hold down one corner as he spread it with his other hand. He ran a finger along a line. He appeared to have found a route with no grades too steep. It was a bit circuitous, and went through Bey Nazar's tribal lands. While it wouldn't affect Nazar directly because he had a position in the khan's retinue, it would send the railroad through the youngster's family lands, making it easier to get their herds to market.

That should please the count, Togym thought a bit resentfully. The southern route would have gone through Togym's lands, which would have provided him with considerable stock in the rail lines and put him in position to become the main beef and mutton supplier for eastern Russia. Now that advantage would go to Nazar's clan. Togym would become weaker as Nazar's clan gained wealth and power. Not a bad trade for a few square miles of land that weren't much good for anything but hunting mountain goats.

Togym looked at Bey Nazar. He looked interested, and that was all that Togym could tell. The kid was getting good at hiding his thoughts. And it occurred to Togym that perhaps Nazar had bribed the Russian cartographer to send the railroad through his clan's lands.

The meeting continued and Togym almost forgot about the "issues with the water table," but not quite.

* * *

As the meeting wrapped up, they set out the route for the next leg of the surveying trip. They would be going almost due east through

35

the southern end of the Ural mountains. Twisting and turning, following the route Ivan had mapped out.

Location: East of Druzhba
Date: June 25, 1637

Ivan Smirnov looked through the transit. As usual, he was miles ahead of the caravan and the news wasn't good. The grade here was too steep. They weren't just going to have to dig, they were going to have to blast, and it was going to set up a choke point for the rail line. A place where just a few men could block the passage of the trains.

It wasn't all bad news. If the khan set up a fort on the top of that hill over there, he would command the pass. And that would make using the rail for most of the route, then moving your goods off the rail to avoid the tariffs more difficult. He would have to stress that advantage in the next conference.

He pulled out his notebook and made a note. Ivan's spelling was esoteric at best, but he knew what he was saying. The notes were more reminders than anything else.

Ivan finished his note and was opening the saddle bag to put the note pad back when he felt the pain. An arrow was protruding from his back between the two lower ribs.

He dropped the note pad, which fell to the ground, and grabbed the pommel of his saddle to keep from falling down. Ivan was a big man and strong. He was also brave and tough. He didn't fall over. Even in pain he was clear thinking enough to know that he had to get back to camp for medical care if he was to have any hope of survival.

He pulled himself onto his horse by force of will as much as by the strength of his arms. He got his hands on the reins, turned the horse and began to ride, the arrow in his back shooting pain through him with every hoofbeat.

Ivan had the vices of his virtues. It didn't occur to him to call his surveying assistants to help. It didn't really occur to him to ask anyone for help. He just turned and rode.

He made it almost a mile before internal bleeding and agony made him lose control of the horse, and the horse wandered without direction for another fifty yards before he fell off, landing on his back and forcing the arrow out through his chest.

In a grove of trees almost forty yards from where Ivan was shot, a man cursed as he watched Ivan, arrow in his back, climb onto the horse and ride away. He'd expected Smirnov to fall dead right there, not to climb onto a horse and ride away. The bastard hadn't even screamed.

Quietly, but quickly, he unstrung his bow and led his horse away. Behind a ridge on the other side of the glade, he mounted up and rode away, carefully avoiding the surveyors.

Gorg Huff & Paula Goodlette

CHAPTER 3: IVAN IS DEAD

Location: Camp East of Druzhba
Date: June 25, 1637

The surveyors had lost track of Ivan and when they got back to camp and learned that he wasn't there, they went looking for Vasilii.

"What is it, Gregor?" Vasilii asked as the scout rode up.

"Colonel Smirnov is missing."

"Missing or just late? When did you last see him?"

"Midafternoon." Gregor didn't own a watch. He was illiterate and in all honesty, not that bright. He could ride well, hold a stick straight up, and follow hand signals. Which was about all Ivan Smirnov wanted in his assistants. Well, he was also possessed of a bovine patience that was another requirement for working for Ivan.

"Where?"

"About six miles that way." Gregor pointed to the southeast.

"What was he doing?"

"Waving that he was done with the reading, and I should go on to the next location."

"And?"

Gregor shrugged. "I went to the next spot and put the stick in place and looked around. He wasn't where he was supposed to be, so I waited."

"How long?"

Gregor visibly struggled with that one. "An hour, maybe."

"An hour?"

"Maybe. The colonel doesn't like to be bothered when he's doing his map making stuff. It's worth a man's job to interrupt him."

"What happened after an hour?"

"I figured I'd misunderstood and he was done for the day. Then I rode back to camp, but he wasn't here."

Vasilii looked at the sun and checked his watch. "All right. Have a horse saddled for me."

He went over to the yurt where Miroslava was sitting on the platform reading a book aloud to Rayana. The story was a Russian translation of "The Hound of the Baskervilles." And while both women knew that Sherlock was a fictional character, they both felt that he was a relative of Miroslava's. Sometimes Vasilii felt the same way, even to the extent of resenting Miroslava's overbearing cousin from England.

"Smirnov has gotten himself lost. I'm taking a couple of the streltzi and riding out to check on him."

Rayana looked up at his statement and said, "You should tell Bey Nazar."

Vasilii grinned. "Not Sultan Togym?"

Rayana sniffed. "Him too, maybe. But Bey Nazar is in charge of the caravan. Sultan Togym is just here for the contracts."

Which was true, though probably not Rayana's only reason. Miroslava had noticed on the first day that Rayana had great respect for Nazar and as soon as they got to Druzhba and hooked up with Togym, she'd made her preference for Nazar pretty plain. She always felt that Nazar should be told anything first.

Still, it wasn't a bad idea. If a bear or bandit got Ivan, it might be wise to have extra backup. And Vasilii didn't want to take all their streltzi with him.

"Should I come?" Miroslava asked.

"It's not a mystery yet. Just a missing surveyor. For all we know, he had too much baijiu and is sleeping it off in a shady glade.

✳ ✳ ✳

Vasilii, Gregor, and Bey Nazar rode out to where Gregor had last seen Ivan Smirnov, trailed by a couple of streltzi and half a dozen of Nazar's men. The route was a bit different from the one that Gregor had taken back to the camp because Gregor had started from a ridge to the right.

They'd gone about five miles, riding cautiously, walking the horses most of the way, when one of Bey Nazar's men pointed.

Vasilii looked and saw a pile of horse droppings. Horses don't usually do their business at a gallop. In fact, they usually stop, do their thing, then wander off. A careful look at the area around the pile showed a hoof mark in the grass and some grass cropped by what was probably a horse, and one in no particular hurry. Following the tracks led to Ivan's stallion, calmly cropping grass.

Bey Nazar rode quickly over and grabbed the reins. Socks didn't object, probably happy enough at the prospect of getting the saddle removed and a nice grooming.

"There's blood on the saddle!" Bey Nazar said before Vasilii got there.

And there was. It was on the back edge, but it was a spray, more as though blood had soaked the back of Ivan's shirt and pants. It was a warm June day, so Ivan's jacket was tied neatly to the back of his saddle. There was blood on it as well, but again not as though it had spread or splattered or even dripped really.

"I wish Miroslava was here," Vasilii said.

"Your concubine?" Nazar asked. "She is attractive, and insightful, as even women can sometimes be. But, really, this is hardly a place for a woman."

"She's Czar Mikhail's detective. The only licensed detective on this side of the Rhine."

There was a smirk in Nazar's eyes that didn't quite touch his lips. "Yes. I'd heard that. If you like, I can send Didar here to fetch her. I would like to see this 'detective' in action."

Everyone could hear the quotes in Nazar's voice and most of the Kazakhs were openly grinning. Especially Didar.

"Actually, that's an excellent idea," Vasilii said. "Gregor, you go with Didar here. Miroslava Holmes is an excellent detective, and a friend of the czarina, but she's not a horsewoman. Wait, let me write her a note."

Miroslava was a contradiction. She still read slowly, but no one could tell because she memorized the page as soon as she saw it. She would receive the note, then read it in her mind's eye as she came to the scene.

"She can read?" Nazar asked. Nazar could read both Arabic and the Kazakh language and struggle through Russian. He'd been educated in one of the best madrasas in the Kazakh Khanate. And this was still a time when Arabic and Islamic scholars were among the best in the world. Vasilii knew that Bernie Zeppi had been surprised by that and that Cass Lowry had flat refused to believe it, but it was true.

"She can read now," Vasilii confirmed, trying to indicate how rapidly Miroslava had learned her letters. He was quite proud of her, and in a way of his role in giving her the opportunity to use her prodigious intellect and odd way of seeing the world. He pulled his notepad from the pocket of his tunic and using the mechanical pencil, he wrote:

"Blood evidence of foul play. Bring kit!"

Then he tore the sheet from the pad, folded it, and handed it to Gregor. "Give this to Lady Holmes and you will probably need to lead her horse."

By the time Miroslava, Didar, and Gregor got back to where they found the horse, Bey Nazar, Vasilii, and party had found the body by backtracking the horse's route. Miroslava looked at the saddle and saw Ivan Smirnov leaning . . . no, hunching over in the saddle, half unconscious. The wound in the left back, near the bottom of the rib cage. The blood seeping out. The wound, the arrow still in it, blocking the flow, slowing the bleeding. Every step of the horse jarring the wound and letting a little more blood flow into his clothing to be wicked by the cloth. There was more bleeding than the saddle showed, but most of it would have been wicked away by his shirt and his pants. "The only blood on the saddle was blood that was transferred from his pants," she said aloud. "I imagine his shirt was soaked."

"It was," said the Kazakh who'd been left to guide them the rest of the way to the body. "Your Vasilii insisted that we not move the body. Didn't even want us to get close to it. Is that some Christian religious thing?"

"No. It is an up-timer thing. It helps in figuring out who committed a crime. The wound was in the back, near the bottom of the rib cage."

"There's a hole in his belly with an arrow sticking out," the Kazakh said, smirking.

Miroslava looked up at the grinning man on the horse. He wasn't lying, but he couldn't be right. Then she had it.

Miroslava wasn't any less egotistic than anyone else, and these days much of her ego was tied in with her ability as a detective. She thought differently than other people, saw things they missed, and missed things they saw. But she was just as human as anyone else, and didn't like being thought incompetent anymore than anyone else does. So she said, "Not when he was on this horse, it wasn't."

Then she climbed back on the old mare that Gregor had led here, and they proceeded to the body.

* * *

As soon as Miroslava saw the body, her suspicions were confirmed. She looked over at the Kazakh and said, "See the shirt around the exit wound? Very little blood. Ivan's heart stopped within seconds of his landing here. Either before he fell off the horse, or right after. It was his landing on his back that drove the arrow out his front. While he was on the horse, he had no wound in front."

After she'd said it, she regretted saying it. After all, everyone here was a suspect. She looked at the body. The blood was tacky, starting to dry. And she had Gregor's time of last seeing Ivan alive. That gave her a fairly precise time window, assuming Gregor was telling the truth. Between two and four hours ago. That at least eliminated Vasilii. He'd been with her in the time window.

She climbed off the horse with some difficulty. Even with the horse being led and her holding onto the pommel, the motion and position of riding a horse wasn't one her body was used to, and it was telling her about it. She got her kit out. The camera she pulled from the saddlebag was a sort of copy of a Folding Autographic Brownie made in Ufa, based on a design developed in Grantville. The film was from the Moscow Dacha and smuggled into Ufa.

Cameras were still rare and film was expensive, but there were three on the trip. Her camera, used for crime scene photographs, Vasilii's, used for whatever he wanted to photograph, usually mountains or people, and Ivan Smirnov's, used to photograph terrain features, usually with at least one surveyor's rod in the picture.

Miroslava had a good eye for detail, but that didn't translate into a good eye for composition. She handed the camera to Vasilii and then told him what to photograph. The film would be sent back to Ufa for development, and the pictures, or copies of them anyway, would be sent back to her here. She had Vasilii take six shots of the body and two of the horse.

But this was no more the murder scene than where they found the horse had been.

"Where was he shot?" Miroslava asked.

"In the back," said Didar, and Miroslava wasn't sure if he didn't understand the question or was laughing at her.

"I mean, where was he when he was shot in the back?" Miroslava clarified her question.

"Unfortunately, we lost his trail about a hundred yards that way," Bey Nazar said, pointing. And he sounded regretful.

"Then have Gregor show us where he was when he was last seen, and we will track him from there," Miroslava said.

No one actually slapped themselves on the head or asked aloud "Why didn't I think of that?" but they might as well have.

"But before we do that, I want to examine the body."

Miroslava slowly and meticulously examined the body from head to foot, having Vasilii photograph everything. She found nuggets of gold in Ivan's lower right tunic pocket. Ivan dressed in the latest styles. That meant his tunic had two upper pockets, one on each breast, and two lower pockets, one at each hip. All the pockets had actual brass zippers. She didn't find the notebook, though she remembered that Ivan had one.

If someone took it, she wondered why. And why not the gold? Ivan also had a six-shot caplock revolver. It hadn't been fired in the last few hours. It was still in his holster, the flap buttoned down. It wasn't a quick draw holster. It was more along the lines of something a military officer would wear, which fit with the man. The other side of the gun belt had two spare six-shot cylinders, both fully loaded.

There was grass on his pants and boots, and on the seat of his trousers, so he'd been sitting in the grass in the last few hours. There was blood soaking down the back of his tunic, and dampening the trousers above the belt, which was tooled leather with a brass buckle.

Finally, she finished her examination, turned over the gold nuggets, the pistol, and pistol belt with the spare cylinders, which were actually worth more, to Bey Nazar. And they went looking for where Gregor had last seen Ivan alive.

*   *   *

After Gregor pointed out the place he'd last seen Ivan, Miroslava had everyone but Vasilii and Nazar stay back. Vasilii knew how to avoid contaminating a crime scene and she couldn't keep Nazar back. He was in charge of the investigation. And besides, these were his tribal lands. His cousin, Sultan Aidar Karimov, was the headman or chief of this band of Kazakhs. Which might or might not mean Aidar had motive. Word was that the tribe was happy the rail line was to go through their lands.

"See the scuff mark?" Miroslava said, then stopped. There it was, on the ground. Ivan's notebook. It was just like Vasilii's, a wood clipboard about two inches wide and five long, with a steel spring clip holding the pages, a clip to hold a mechanical pencil that was lying next to the clipboard. What Bernie called "geek chic," because between the mechanical pencil and the clipboard it cost more than a new set of clothing.

Miroslava pointed at the clipboard. "Take a picture of that, Vasilii." She looked around and noted the position of the clipboard and hoof marks in the grass. She saw everything, but the mind needs references and Miroslava wasn't a scout. She didn't know what a horse's hoof print planted just so meant, nor how it differed from a hoof print planted six inches to the left.

She looked back at the group of Kazakhs and called, "Didar, come here."

Bey Nazar looked at her, then shrugged and waved for Didar to come. Didar rode up and she waved for him to stop. "See those hoof prints next to the notebook?"

Didar made a guess about what a notebook was, climbed down from his horse, and signaled it to stay where it was. He trusted the horse to stay more than he trusted the strange woman to hold it. Then he carefully walked over to examine the hoof prints. "Yesss!" he hissed. He turned to Bey Nazar speaking in Kazakh. "The witch is right. Colonel Smirnov pulled himself onto his horse here. He didn't mount properly. He pulled himself on. Well trained horse. Most would have shifted, but this one let the man pull himself up. He had to be already wounded. No fit man would mount that way."

Nazar nodded. "He says that the colonel mounted badly, that he had to already be wounded."

Miroslava remembered the colonel's horse. A saddlebag was opened. But only one. "Did anyone open the saddlebag on Colonel Smirnov's horse?"

"No one touched it." Bey Nazar sounded offended.

Miroslava had no idea why. She might not be a scout, but she could tell where the horse was standing. The saddlebag was opened, the notepad on the ground. He was putting the notebook away when he was shot. The horse's position and the notebook gave her Smirnov's position when the arrow hit him. He was facing the horse. And that, along with the entry and exit wounds, told her the direction the arrow was traveling when it hit him. She turned, backtracking the arrow, and the closest hiding place was a stand of trees about forty yards away.

Miroslava started walking that way.

Vasilii, smiling, followed.

Bey Nazar and Didar looked at each other and hurried to catch up. "Where are you going?" Nazar asked.

"The shooter was in that stand of trees."

Didar looked at the trees, looked back at where the horse had been, and realized she was right. He made a gesture of warding off evil and followed.

In the grove, they found scuffed boot prints. They couldn't even get an approximate size of the man. There were also scuffed hoof prints of a good sized horse, by the distance between the hooves.

Vasilii took pictures of everything. They collected the notebook, the body, Smirnov's horse, and then they went back to camp.

* * *

Back in camp, Sultan Togym was told what they had found. "Are you accusing a Kazakh of this?" He was trying to sound outraged and Vasilii thought he was, at least a little. But mostly he was worried.

"We aren't accusing anyone," Vasilii said. "Just reporting the facts. He was shot with an arrow. The arrow was still in his body when he was found, though it was broken at the fletching from when he fell out of the saddle. It was handmade in the Kazakh style. He was standing by his horse when he was shot, and he pulled himself onto the back of the animal and rode some distance before lack of blood sent him unconscious, and he fell onto his back on the ground, driving the arrow through his body and breaking the fletching."

"If he rode away, how do you know where he was shot?"

"Because his woman is a witch!" Bey Nazar said in Kazakh.

"Speak Russian, Nazar," Togym said.

"Because Vasilii's woman is a witch," Nazar said in quite good Russian.

"No. I am a detective," Miroslava said.

"What's a detective?" Togym asked.

"Someone who detects how a crime was committed," Miroslava said.

"Sounds like a witch to me!" Didar muttered.

"The khan will have to be informed," Togym said. "No one is to leave camp until we have heard from the khan."

"Czar Mikhail will have to be informed," Vasilii said, more to hear how Togym would respond than for any other reason. Vasilii knew he didn't need to send anyone to inform the czar. He had one of the new, and precious, tubed radios in his gear. On the other hand, he did need to get the film back to Ufa.

"You are in the Kazakh Khanate now, not Russia!" Sultan Togym blurted.

"Actually, we're in both," Bey Nazar said. "You do recall that the khan signed the constitution and Kazakh is now a state in the United Sovereign States of Russia."

"A *sovereign* state. The investigation of a crime in the *sovereign* state of Kazakh is the province of the khan, not the czar!"

"Even the death of a Russian officer?" Bey Nazar seemed to be intentionally needling the sultan.

"Anyone!" Togym insisted.

"I take it that you don't want me sending the crime scene photos back to Ufa to be developed?" Vasilii asked.

"Crime scene photos?" Togym asked.

That entailed a whole new explanation. Which Vasilii gave as calmly as he could, pointing out that the pictures would no doubt aid whoever the khan assigned to investigate the crime.

Togym rubbed his eyes and said, "Not yet. We will wait and see what the khan says."

* * *

The sun had set by the time the meeting was over, but as soon as they got back to the mobile yurt that was their home away from home, Vasilii set up the radio and called the network of stations. The message would reach Ufa in fifteen minutes or so.

CHAPTER 4: A CASE FOR THE KHAN

Location: Camp of the Khan
Date: June 28, 1637

The dispatch rider was exhausted, and his horse was worse. This did not bode well for the contents of the dispatch.

Jangir took the dispatch and began to read. The signals didn't lie. This could be a disaster. "Get me a good horse and three spares, the same for a troop of ten men. We ride as soon as we are equipped."

It took some time and some argument, but he was the khan. They rode out that night and made twenty miles before stopping for the night.

Location: Camp East of Druzhba
Date: July 2, 1637

The khan and his men were exhausted, and they had lost five horses on the trip. But that didn't stop him from reading Togym the riot act.

After quite a few heated words in Kazakh, he turned to Vasilii. "You have a radio?"

"Yes, Salqam-Jangir Khan."

"Good. I need to talk to Mikhail."

"Our radio can send voice, but several of the stations on the route can only send data, specifically teletype. So I will have to send the messages in code." The teletype machines were Russian made with Cyrillic letters.

"It will do. I assume you told him what happened."

"Yes, Salqam-Jangir Khan."

"What did he say?"

"That it was your state and he trusted you to get to the bottom of it," Vasilii said, which was close enough. Mikhail suspected that someone in Salqam-Jangir Khan's court was trying to break up the union before it had a good chance to form.

There were now four states. Kazakh, Ufa, Kazan, and one of the noble states that had formed since Mikhail's arrival in Ufa. General Shein was still sitting with a fence post up his bum, and most of the Ural states—that is the states that had formed east of the Volga and west of the Ural mountains—were following his lead. If they lost Kazakh, the largest state so far in the union, they were dead. So Vasilii was to support Salqam-Jangir Khan even if he laid the blame on a clearly innocent Russian. It was just too important to do anything else. At the same time, he was to subtly encourage Salqam-Jangir Khan to find and punish the guilty party, especially if it was one of his, because Czar Mikhail was going to be getting heat from the hard liners in his court.

Mikhail was fully aware that those were conflicting instructions, but he had "every confidence in you, Vasilii."

"I thought that was what he would say." Jangir Khan grinned a boyish grin, demonstrating his youth for all to see. He was very young for his role. "Mikhail is a wise leader. Wise enough to give up a little power for the welfare and stability of his country."

Vasilii noticed that he was looking at both Togym and Nazar when he said that. That surprised Vasilii a little. So far on the trip, Nazar had seemed in favor of the khanate becoming a state. And Togym was the one who had been fairly openly upset by it. Well, worried about the long term consequences, anyway.

"Very well, Vasilii, we will go have a chat with Czar Mikhail."

✻ ✻ ✻

For over an hour Vasilii dotted and dashed his way through a conversation between Jangir Khan and Czar Mikhail. When Mikhail pointed out that the only private detective in Russia was right here in camp, Jangir Khan asked Vasilii what he was talking about. And Vasilii got to tell him about Miroslava and the art of detection and crime scene photos.

"Wait a moment," Jangir Khan said, then yelled, "Cousin, have a dispatch rider take the crime scene film to Ufa as fast as he can ride." He turned back to Vasilii. "So this bar girl thinks in a unique way, and sees things others miss. Go on."

Vasilii went on.

When the telegraphing was done for the evening, Jangir Khan clapped Vasilii on the shoulder. "I think I will borrow your bar girl." He didn't say it like it was a request. Nor did he specify what use he was going to put Miroslava to.

"She isn't a bar girl anymore, Jangir Khan. Nor is she a thing to be borrowed. She is Miroslava Holmes, Consulting Detective. You can hire her to investigate if you choose to, but be aware she isn't hired to catch an individual. She is hired to find the truth. And truth is what you will get. Not the story you might want, but the truth."

Vasilii knew he was harping on the "truth," but he wanted Jangir Khan to understand.

"Well, the truth is what I want. I will hire the consulting detective, and we will see what she detects."

Location: Camp East of Druzhba
Date: July 4, 1637

For Miroslava, the date had no significance. Well, it didn't have all that much for Vasilii either. Their July 4 was April 17, the day Czar Mikhail and Salqam-Jangir Khan signed the Constitution of the USSR. So, rather than eating hot dogs and setting off bottle rockets, she was reading through Colonel Ivan Smirnov's notebook.

Or trying to.

Ivan didn't encrypt his notebook. Not exactly. But Ivan had been a lazy man with an excellent memory. The notebook didn't have notes so much as reminders, metaphorical bits of string tied around metaphorical fingers. Things that meant something to Ivan, but not necessarily to anyone else. She was sitting on the wooden platform of the *khibitkha* next to the entrance of the yurt. It was, after all, a bright, sunny July day with a sapphire blue sky and a cool breeze from the northeast.

None of that impinged on Miroslava. She was immersed in the footprints of the mind of Ivan Smirnov. She did have an advantage in her search over Miss Marple, Quincy ME, or even Cousin Sherlock, as she was coming to think of Conan Doyle's fictional detective.

That advantage was the fact that she'd spent most of her life illiterate. She knew about memory tags because she used them herself. Their function was less to cause you to remember something, more to bring something you remembered already to your attention. That was what the string and rock and bits of pine cone in her boxes back in Room 22B, Ufa Dacha were for, and that was what the "notes" in this notebook were for.

So she was learning what a note meant on a page, and guessing that it meant something similar on another page. And, so far, she was making not much progress at all.

Location: Salqam-Jangir Khan's Yurt, Camp East of Druzhba
Date: July 4, 1637

"Have a seat, Vasilii." Jangir Khan waved to cushions. "What do you know of the Zunghars?"

"Very little."

"They are a related people, our cousins in a way. But they have recently converted to Mahayana Buddhism. Their leader, Erdeni Batur, thinks that he can restore the empire of Genghis Khan."

"If you don't mind my asking, why us and not him? Why join the United Sovereign States of Russia, not the restored Mongol empire?"

"Two reasons. First, he wasn't asking. He didn't ask us to join his nation, but instead tried to conquer us. And second, there is no constitution that ensures religious freedom for Muslims in his restored Mongol empire. Nor any of the other agreements I got as I sat in the constitutional convention." Jangir Khan shook his head and added a third reason.

"There is very little about us in the encyclopedias from Grantville and what there is is mostly from the Soviet period. But one thing is clear. Unless history changes drastically, it will be the cultures of the west that dominate the future, not the culture of China or the Mongols. If my people are ever to be more than a footnote in that future, we will have to learn western ways and western tools. You, your people, can offer that. Erdeni Batur cannot."

Vasilii nodded his agreement, not at all sure where this was going. He knew some of it from the constitutional convention. He'd even met and talked with the khan a few times. But he had no idea what he was doing here.

"Erdeni Batur is not going to be convinced of that. Neither is Zhu Youjian, the emperor of China."

"China's a little far off, Highness, isn't it?" The words Vasilii used were "*Siyatelstvo Vashe*," a Russian phrase that translated, roughly, as "Illustrious Highness." It was what had been agreed to, a little informally, as the form of address of state rulers, so in one sense it was actually closer to "governor" than "king."

The young khan of the state of Kazakh saw Vasilii's confusion and grinned. "By now, even without radios, word of our joining the USSR will have reached Erdeni Batur. In another month, it will reach Beijing. And you're right. Zhu Youjian will read it in a report and ignore it. Especially with up-timer knowledge arriving from the coast, which is much closer. But the governors of his western provinces will take note and possibly take action. And if the railroad goes through, if even word of the railroad reaches the east, that note, will become interest, even fear.

"What will Erdeni Batur do then? Robbed of his restored Mongol empire, and threatened by western influence arriving by train from Shavgar, Ufa, and soon enough, Moscow and the USE. Will he say 'oh well, maybe next time?' Will he cower in fear at the new might of the USSR? I don't think so. Erdeni Batur isn't the cowering kind."

"But he has treaties with Russia," Vasilii said. "Well, had treaties, before Czar Mikhail escaped to Ufa. And he's been actively encouraging his people to take up crafts and trades. Encouraging a uniform code of laws. A railroad and peaceful relations between his people and yours would give him access to up-timer tech that he's going to need in dealing with China."

"Either that, or it's a threat to his power," Jangir Khan said. "My problem is I don't know which way he's going to interpret the situation. But I suspect that he's going to see our joining the USSR as a threat rather than an opportunity, and if he does, he could come in now to try and crush it."

"Can he do that?"

"Maybe. His hold on the Zunghars is not solid. Partly because he isn't a true heir to Genghis Khan, at least not by blood, and several of the Zunghar tribal leaders are. But our threat might just be enough to make them put aside their pride and accept his leadership."

This, Vasilii thought not for the first time, was way above his pay grade. This was above Bernie's pay grade. It belonged in the czar's in-basket, not with a steam engineer. "What do you want me to do about all this, *Siyatelstvo Vashe?*"

"If the alliance, which is still politically fragile, comes apart, the Zunghar are going to ravage my people. Czar Mikhail can't have it look like I am ignoring the murder of one of his nobles. It would insure that Shein stayed out. It might even cause Kazan to reconsider. And I can't have the czar's representative—" He pointed at Vasilii. "—overturning our laws or going about questioning my nobles. I wish we had an up-timer or a Chinese ambassador handy, but we don't. The best we have is your—"

The khan paused, clearly looking for a polite way of saying what everyone had been thinking since they started on this mission, that

Miroslava was just Vasilii's doxie, a fling who had been given pseudo status to justify Vasilii's bringing along his bed partner.

"Miroslava is indeed my . . . intimate companion, Highness. But that's not all she is. She is independent. As independent as you could want. She has solved several murders and thefts in Ufa, and captured villains in Kazan."

"I don't care if she's independent or your puppet. I just can't have her *seen* as your puppet."

"I don't know how to do that, Highness," Vasilii admitted.

"I do. But you're not going to like it. I understand you bought her contract from the brothel keeper in Ufa for . . . what was it? . . . fifteen rubles?"

"Yes," Vasilii said, not liking it at all.

"I will pay you twenty," Jangir Khan said as though it was a done deal.

"No." Vasilii didn't say it loudly, but he did say it firmly.

"You're going to bargain? Very well. Twenty-five, but don't get greedy."

"No. Not for any price," Vasilii said, but he felt he had to explain, or at least try. "Miroslava is very literal minded. In a very real sense, if you buy her contract, it will be as though you had bought her. More importantly, it would be as though I sold her. I won't do that. Not for anything.

"If she wants her contract, she can have it. In fact, I've already offered to give it to her more than once. But I won't sell it to anyone else for any reason."

"Your girl isn't the only one who's literal minded in this, Vasilii. As long as you own her contract, my nobles will never trust anything she says. I need this and so does the United Sovereign States of Russia. You said that you offered to give her her contract?"

"Yes. The first time was the night I bought it. She refused and I didn't understand why."

The khan looked surprised. "Really? You didn't understand why someone raised to be a slave would find freedom frightening? You say Miroslava is literal minded. She's not the only one. But, frightening or not, she is going to have to accept her freedom. Ask her, Vasilii. Put it to her as a problem to solve."

* * *

Miroslava was still working on the notebook when Vasilii came in. He told her what Jangir Khan wanted and that he'd said no. Miroslava was surprised to find that she was pleased that Vasilii didn't want to sell her contract. Then Vasilii explained the khan's reasoning. As long as her contract belonged to him, the Kazakh nobles wouldn't believe she was independent. That her conclusions were her own.

"Then if the khan owned my contract, the conclusions would be his, not mine."

Vasilii nodded agreement.

"Then I will buy my contract."

"I've already offered to give you your contract."

"No!" Miroslava didn't know why she said that. Especially, she didn't know why she said that so quickly and automatically. She waved Vasilii to silence while she tried to work it out. Miroslava had gone from child to slave to contracted employee. What she had never been, or been allowed to consider being, was an independent person.

Miroslava was just as analytical with herself as she was with everything else. She realized that she was afraid of being independent. That wasn't anything unique to her. Almost no one in Russia was truly independent, and of those who were, almost none of them were women, and almost none of those had been born to a peasant family. There was only one person she knew of who fit all those categories, and that was Anya.

Miroslava knew she could never be Anya. Anya was beautiful, but she wasn't strange. Miroslava was definitely strange. Strange people were disliked and attacked. For Miroslava, her owner or the owner of her contract was a vital necessity. They were the person who told her what to do and not do to avoid being attacked. They were also, directly or indirectly, the person who fended off those attacks. Madam Drozdov through the bouncers, and Vasilii through the Dacha.

And those attacks would come. Because, for Miroslava, being strange wasn't optional. It wasn't something she could avoid. She was afraid of owning her contract because she needed someone to tell her how to act normal and to protect her when she couldn't.

But that wasn't all. In fact, that was basically the conclusion she'd come to when Vasilii had first offered to give her her contract.

But now there was something new.

It wasn't that she needed *someone* to own her contract.

She wanted—maybe needed—*Vasilii* to own her contract.

That was why she'd been pleased that Vasilii refused to sell it to the khan.

Was this what normal people meant when they talked about love?

And if so, why would she love Vasilii? He wasn't skilled at sex. He was learning, but not particularly skilled. He wasn't handsome. Not ugly, really, but not especially handsome. He was nice to her, and though Miroslava couldn't be sure of such things, he seemed to like her.

Love, if this was love, seemed a very silly thing to feel.

And none of that solved the problem. The khan and the czar needed her to be an independent detective. Not the czar's Holmes or the khan's Holmes, but her own Holmes. And that terrified her.

But the khan was right.

Two things had to happen. One, this case had to be solved. And two, it had to be solved by a person that both sides would accept as independent and honest.

And that was her.

Vasilii was going to have to sell the khan her contract. And the khan, not Vasilii, was going to have to give it to her. If she was beholden to anyone here it had to be the khan, not Vasilii.

She explained all that to Vasilii.

CHAPTER 5: MIROSLAVA'S CONTRACT

Location: Camp East of Druzhba
Date: July 6, 1637

The ceremony was public, with the Kazakhs gathered around and watching Salqam-Jangir Khan count out the equivalent of twenty-five rubles and give them to Vasilii, and Vasilii gave him Miroslava's contract. Then, at the khan's instruction, Miroslava handed him her ID, the little folder that had her photograph and was printed with a five pointed star. The folder that listed her name as Miroslava Holmes. He showed it to the Kazakhs, then he gave it back to her, turned to the crowd, and spoke in a light baritone. "Czar Mikhail didn't make Miroslava Holmes his with this. It calls her a private detective, not a police detective or a streltzi detective. But some might worry that she is still more loyal to the czar than to Us."

He brought out a vellum sheet with gold filigree and beautiful calligraphy that, in its turn, gave Miroslava Holmes the status of private detective in the Sovereign State of Kazakh.

"But if her findings are to be trusted, they must not be findings for me, anymore than findings for Czar Mikhail. So, Miroslava Holmes, Private Detective, I give to you your contract and hire you with it, to find the true murderer of Colonel Ivan Smirnov and bring them before me for my judgment."

* * *

Miroslava then had to stand there and accept the congratulations of the powers of the khan's court, at least those of them that were here.

Bey Nazar's were warm and heartfelt. Sultan Togym's were grudging. Nazar's cousin, Aidar, whose clan territory this was, were congratulatory, but distant. Togym's retainers were almost surly.

* * *

That night in the yurt, Miroslava didn't know what to do. If she was still a bar girl and Vasilii was a customer, she would know what to do. If Vasilii owned her contract, she would know what to do. Having sex would be her job, her contractual obligation. One that she enjoyed, but still her job.

But in spite of what Vasilii said during the case of the spy that got away, Miroslava wasn't at all sure that women who were neither prostitutes or married actually had sex. And Miroslava needed rules to tell her how to behave.

This owning your own contract business didn't have enough rules.

So Miroslava slept on her side of the bed and Vasilii on his.

Location: Ufa Dacha, Photo Lab
Date: July 6, 1637

Four days of hard riding had brought the courier from the camp to Ufa and the film was given first priority in the Dacha photo lab. There were now two rolls of twenty negatives, each relating to the murder and another two rolls taken by Vasilii, as well as the three rolls taken by Ivan Smirnov which, according to the latest radio message, Miroslava wanted in her search for motive.

There was a lock on the photo lab's door. A sort of a lock. It was a heavy wooden unit, painted red on the outside part. When it was latched, there was a red bar in front of the door, both to keep it from being opened and to warn everyone that the darkroom was in use.

Detective Sergeant Pavel Baranov wanted these photos ASAP, and Maksim Borisovich Vinnikov was pacing the hall outside the darkroom waiting for the film. Finally, the door opened and a stack of still slightly damp photographs were brought out. "These are the crime scene pictures. I'm still working on the rest."

* * *

Maksim took the photos to the kremlin, where the streltzi "cop shop" was located.

Pavel was at his desk when Maksim came in. He was struggling through a witness report on a murder on Irina Way. It wasn't a question of who did the murder, but of whether it was murder or self

67

defense, and Maksim knew it was going to be a tough call. But the brand new magistrate of Ufa wanted Pavel's input.

Pavel gratefully put the report aside and started going through the pictures.

There was one of the body, turned over so you could see the fletching on the arrow. "Miroslava will want a blow up of this part." He drew a circle on the photo with a grease pencil, then took the next picture. There were several other places where he pointed out a salient feature and said that the lab should do blowups. It would take another day and several complaints from the staff of the photo lab before Pavel was satisfied and the images were put on the horse of a dispatch rider and sent back.

In the meantime, the investigation wasn't exactly on hold, but was delayed.

Location: Camp East of Druzhba
Date: July 7, 1637

Vasilii was in the cab of the steam tractor along with the driver and the fireman. It had been unhooked from the *khibitkha* and was instead pushing a bulldozer blade that was cutting a half inch of soil on each pass. They were making a road bed as Kazakhs looked on in amazement. More amazement than Vasilii was convinced was warranted. There was only the one, and as powerful as it was, half a dozen Fresno scrapers pulled by horses or oxen could do as well in terms of what the "bulldozer rig" could do. And the Kazakhs had a lot of oxen and a hell of a lot of horses. Not to mention massive herds of sheep and goats.

Here was a huge source of food, wool, leather, and other such animal based products for Russia, especially eastern Russia, but even for western Russia centered around Moscow, with the addition of a rail line to connect the Ufa River and, by way of the Aral Sea, the Syr Darya River. Even more, he guessed, if the rail line went directly to Shavgar as Ivan's latest maps said it should. He was sorry about Ivan. Jaroslav Vinokurov, who'd arrived two days ago, was competent, but not nearly as skilled as Ivan had been. Easier to deal with, but not as skilled.

The tractor pushed the heavy iron bulldozer into a boulder, and the whole tractor jerked, as the blade broke the huge rock in two. That wasn't something a team of oxen was going to do.

While the delay continued, the camp was being turned into something of a permanent settlement. Of course, among the Kazakhs, that distinction was pretty fluid. The longer they stayed in one place, the more permanent it became. The tractor was just speeding up the process a bit.

Vasilii wished the solving of this case could be sped up.

Oddly enough, because of the nature of their relationship, Miroslava had always been the one to initiate intimacy. Partly because their roles were such that Vasilii would have felt like he was forcing her if he initiated. But now she wasn't starting things and Vasilii was afraid that it was because she didn't want to, and now that she owned her contract, didn't have to.

The truth was, Vasilii was a geek of the first water, as Bernie said. He wasn't good at romance and his family hadn't arranged anything for him because he had several older brothers—or at least he had

had before Sheremetev took over the government and his family found themselves on the wrong side. So Vasilii didn't know how he was supposed to act.

Location: Wilds of Kazakh Lands
Date: July 7, 1637

Jaroslav Vinokurov looked at the land and was confused. It was nice enough land, mostly open plains, rich, green and full of high summer grass. There was a herd of cattle in the distance with a team of Kazakh herdsmen on horses watching over them. There were a few stands of trees, but no indication of flooding or runoff that he could see.

According to Ivan Smirnov's notes, the groundwater should be high here, such that in the rainy season this area would turn into a bog that the railroad would sink into. But Jaroslav wasn't seeing any indications of it. It could be because Ivan Smirnov was—had been— a better geologist than Jaroslav, but, damn it, he wasn't *that* much better. Maybe it was something that Jaroslav would have missed, but not something that he couldn't see after it was pointed out.

On the other hand, he couldn't imagine how Ivan could have been wrong about something like this.

Something was wrong.

He turned to his first assistant, Stefania. "Do you see it?"

"Nope!" Stefania was in pants. And not even the pseudo dresses that were all the rage in Grantville and increasingly in Ufa. Stefania was wearing leather britches tight enough to display every curve. She also wore a six-shot revolver quite openly on her hip. She had a nose that had been broken in the past, and was missing a tooth on the left side of her mouth. "And if I don't see it, it ain't there."

A survey team consisted of at least two people, and usually four or five. You needed someone on the level-transit and someone on the surveying rod. But you also needed soil and rock samples, notes on the location of groves of trees, rivers, creeks, and dry creek beds. Especially for something like a railroad or canal route. Because you needed to estimate the changes in the land over the seasons and over time in general.

By the late twentieth century, it was mostly science. But even with the knowledge of the up-timers transmitted through the Dacha in the first half of the seventeenth century, it was still an art. And artists don't always concede the abilities of other artists, especially irritating asshole artists like Ivan Smirnov.

"Ivan was good. You have to admit that, Stef."

"Not as good as everyone thought he was, and certainly not as good as he thought he was."

"Bad enough to see a bog out there if there wasn't one. And not some dinky ass bog, but a long bog that would force the rail line to go over a hundred miles out of its way."

"Fine. It's not there, and he wasn't quite dumb enough to imagine it." Stefania looked at the plain again and shook her head. "That just means he was lying."

"Why would he lie?" Jaroslav asked, and then knew the answer. *To divert the railroad.*

He looked at Stefania, and she was looking at him. "But why would he want to divert the railroad? Why would he care?"

"That's a question for the Holmes," Jaroslav said.

And Stefania grimaced. She didn't approve of bar girls. And she really didn't approve of bar girls who got promoted to almost nobility in Russia and Kazakh. Stefania knew that Kazakh was now a state in the USSR, but it still felt like it was a foreign land.

"I don't know why you disapprove of the Holmes?"

"Because they have sex for money. And because some men think we're *all* bar girls. *All* for sale."

"Granted, but that's not their fault. In the case of the Holmes, even the having sex for money wasn't her fault. She was a slave back in Nizhny Novgorod and under contract in Ufa."

"I don't care!" Stefania said succinctly.

Jaroslav shook his head. "Let's get back to camp. Before I report that Ivan Smirnov lied about a bog, I want to dig a well and learn the level of the groundwater."

Location: Camp East of Druzhba
Date: July 8, 1637

Miroslava was frustrated and irritated. Partly that was because she was used to having sex on a regular basis, and of cuddling up to Vasilii at night, and she missed it. Partly it was because she was not having much success with deciphering Ivan Smirnov's notes. She had parts of it, but not the vital bits. Something happened on the eighteenth of June, something he was excited about, but she couldn't be sure. It was nowhere near where he found the potential bog a couple of days later.

For the next three days, Miroslava worried over Ivan's notes. Vasilii talked politics with the khan and his nobles, and Jaroslav and Stefania had a well dug in the wilderness.

Location: Camp East of Druzhba
Date: July 11, 1637

The dispatch rider had a heavy satchel, and he'd changed horses several times. The radio stations were, for now, doubling as pony express remount stations. Radio for anything it could carry, and pony express for the rest.

Vasilii was sitting with Miroslava, going through the photos.

"Why did he blow this up?" Miroslava asked, handing him the blow up of the fletching.

"Rifling!" Vasilii said, grinning. Miroslava liked that grin. It was full of enthusiasm and it had been missing for the last few days. "Fletching is perhaps not quite as unique and unfakeable as rifling, but it's close. Like a signature. Whoever made this arrow signed his work and Kazakh archers make their own arrows. It's a matter of pride."

Miroslava sniffed. She wasn't all that impressed with rifling. She knew and understood that it identified the weapon, but in the murders at the Happy Bottom, it had led the case astray to the serious detriment of a man who wasn't guilty of being anything worse than a jerk.

"It will tell us who made the arrow, not who shot it, unless the shooter is incredibly stupid."

"And how would the shooter get the arrow?"

Vasilii was aware of the dangers of circumstantial evidence, but he still trusted it more than Miroslava did.

"The same way Ivan Grigoriyevich Shkuro got the sniper rifle, steal it."

"Still, we need to find out who uses arrows like this," Vasilii said and Miroslava agreed. Vasilii went looking for the owner of the arrows and Miroslava went back to looking at pictures. Especially the pictures of a small mountain stream in the Kazakh lands. It was a pretty enough place, she guessed, but the pictures weren't, it seemed to her, meant to convey its beauty.

* * *

Bey Nazar professed not to know who the arrow belonged to, but he seemed a little too pleased that Vasilii was interested.

"That was very clever of you. We should have seen it ourselves. After all, our people intentionally make the fletching on our arrows unique, so that we can identify a kill in a hunt."

Vasilii left the meeting feeling like the Kazakhs would have checked the fletching as a matter of course if they were running the investigation.

* * *

"The fletching belongs to Nurken Usenov," Sultan Togym said, and his voice was that of a man informing the doctor that she should go ahead and cut off his leg. "I can't believe he would do such a thing.

He is a good man and loyal, not a plotter or an assassin. Something must be . . . But, no. There is the evidence."

"Don't turn him over to the torturers just yet, Sultan Togym. Miroslava already solved a case where the murderer framed an innocent by using his weapon. I'm not saying that's the case here, but we also need motive and opportunity, and even that's not the same as proof. On the other hand, please quietly put him under a watch. I don't want him leaving camp until this is resolved."

"You?" Togym sneered a bit now. "I thought it was the Holmes that was in charge of the investigation. And you don't even own her contract anymore."

Vasilii bit back his response and took a breath. "She is and I don't, but I still help her with her investigations. You can confirm it with her if you want to, but have the man watched."

* * *

Miroslava looked up to see a bedraggled and dirty crew of Russians and Kazakhs approaching the yurt on wheels. They had dirt from head to toe, and muddy boots. Most of them peeled off to get cleaned up, or so she hoped, but two climbed the steps to the wood platform on which the yurt was built. The woman stood back, not so much as though she was giving the man precedence, but as though she didn't want to get too close to Miroslava. It wasn't an uncommon reaction and Miroslava ignored it. Well, pretended to ignore it. Pretended so well she almost convinced herself.

In the meantime, the man, Jaroslav Vinokurov, squatted next to the chair Miroslava was sitting in, going over the pictures and Ivan's notebook.

"There is no bog!" Jaroslav said quietly, but intensely. "We dug down almost forty feet before our feet got wet. If the place turned into a bog in the wet season, the water table would be within ten feet of the grass. That gives Sultan Togym a motive."

It did give Togym a motive. Moving the railroad from his lands to Nazar's was going to make it much more difficult for Togym to profit from the railroad. Nazar's clan would get the stock and the improved trade with Russia which would make Sultan Togym's lands into a backwater. He would have to do a cattle drive to get to a rail head to sell beef, mutton, and cheese, and to buy guns, lathes and the other tools of modern industrial life. If he realized that Ivan had falsified the evidence to . . . But how would he realize?

Miroslava suddenly knew the answer. Well a big part of the answer. There were some things she needed to check. But she could check them readily enough with a radio message to Ufa.

If the khan owned her contract, she would go to the khan, tell him her results, and let him settle the matter the way he chose. If the czar owned her contract, she would do the same thing, because the czar wanted the khan to settle the matter without national interference.

If Vasilii owned her contract, which she wished he did, well, she'd ask him and he'd probably tell her to do it the same way. But Miroslava owned her contract, so she decided to do it the way a detective in a novel would do it, like Miss Marple. In public.

Miroslava grinned then, and it was a wide grin and just a little bit sly, though Miroslava wasn't aware of that. "Rayana, go to Bey Nazar and tell him I need to speak to the khan tomorrow afternoon. I need Sultan Togym to be there and whichever of his men owns the arrow found in Ivan Smirnov's back. And we'll want Bey Nazar there too, and his cousin, Sultan Aidar, and as many other nobles of the khan's court as are available."

The nobles had been arriving in dribs and drabs since the khan got here. There were quite a few by now.

"You should be there too, Jaroslav and Stefania, to tell the khan what you found."

Location: Gorchakov Residence, Ufa
Date: July 11, 1637

Brandy Bates Gorchakov took the telegram from the runner and read. It was long for a telegram and informed her how much effect discovering a gold mine on the railroad route would have.

She put that together with the rumors over the last little while, especially since Ivan Smirnov's death, then went to see Czar Mikhail. The czar wasn't particularly concerned about the stock price in Ufa. He was much more concerned about a clear and speedy resolution of Ivan's murder and one that didn't disrupt relations with his largest and first state.

"Tell her what she wants to know, Brandy," Czar Mikhail said, "and I hope the truth is the right answer."

Brandy, putting together Miroslava's radio message, the rumors about gold, and her knowledge of stock manipulation from

Grantville after the Ring of Fire, sent Miroslava a description of "pump and dump" stock manipulation.

CHAPTER 6: THE RESOLUTION BARBECUE

Location: Camp East of Druzhba
Date: July 12, 1637

It wasn't exactly going to be a barbecue, but it was going to come pretty close, Vasilii thought as he looked around. The Kazakh were a herder people and were as prone to that sort of meal as any Texas cattle baron Vasilii had ever read about. So there would be a cow on a spit rotating over a smoky fire while it was dabbed with sauces. The nature of the sauces would be a bit different. The tomato hadn't yet made it this far inland.

And the outfits were going to be different. No ten gallon hats, and six-shooters were still rare. Sultan Togym sported one, but Bey Nazar wore an *aldaspan*, which was basically a scimitar made by Kazakh smiths. And his form of side weapon was a lot more common than Sultan Togym's. Salqam-Jangir Khan had a down-time made PPK with smokeless powder rounds, just like Miroslava and Vasilii.

The clothing was mostly wool felt embroidered in complex patterns with brightly colored threads. Conspicuous consumption of the very rich was as much on display as in any salon in Moscow.

The fact that they were in the open under a sapphire blue sky with only a few puffy white clouds didn't change that, nor did the fact that they were surrounded by gently rolling hills covered in tall grass just starting to turn from green to gold.

The smells of the roasting meat and spices had Vasilii ready to drool. Or would have, if he knew what was going on. As it was, he was almost too nervous to be hungry. Miroslava had called this party with the agreement of the khan, and Vasilii hadn't been consulted.

The khan waved a hand and a large man shouted in Kazakh. By now Vasilii got the gist. "Gather round, all you who have business before the khan."

"You wished to address Us and certain members of Our court," Salqam-Jangir Khan said in Russian, then repeated in Kazakh. "What have you to tell us?"

Vasilii saw Nurken Usenov, the Kazakh warrior whose arrow had been sticking in Ivan's back, flanked by two of the khan's men. Sultan Togym also had an escort, though he wasn't disarmed as his man was. Both were looking at Miroslava with resentment in their eyes. They could see where the evidence pointed as well as anyone else.

Bey Nazar was working hard not to look pleased, but he wasn't carrying it off, not quite. And that bothered Vasilii because by now word was all over the camp that Ivan had rigged the maps and the rail line was probably going to end up going through Togym's lands after all. Not that it would do Togym any good.

"This case was more complicated than it looked," Miroslava said in Russian and a man standing next to the khan translated into Kazakh almost as she spoke. "But the real delay was in the availability of the evidence. I had to wait for the pictures of the fletching and some other pictures that Ivan and Vasilii took before I could figure out what it was all about."

Bey Nazar was looking rather like a cat with a bowl of cream now. Not just pleased, but superior and pleased. And Togym was looking like a condemned criminal intent on facing his death with dignity.

Then Vasilii noticed that Nazar's tribal chieftain was looking disappointed. That made excellent sense. So why was Nazar happy?

"It was indeed about Ivan Smirnov shifting the direction of the railroad," Miroslava said, "but not just about that. Politics were involved as well." She looked at Sultan Togym, and said, "But so was gold."

Togym looked confused. As confused as Vasilii felt.

Miroslava continued. "Everyone assumed that Ivan just moved the railroad on a whim, or because he didn't like Sultan Togym. I'm sure that Ivan didn't like Sultan Togym, but Ivan didn't like anyone very much, and he did love his maps. Like anyone who is very good at something, Ivan Smirnov took extraordinary pride in the accuracy of his maps."

Now she was getting considering looks from the crowd. The evidence said that Togym had ordered his man to kill Ivan. It was possible that the man acted on his own, but that was as far as the possibilities went. So it had to be about Ivan not liking Togym.

"No, for Ivan to produce a false map, it had to be important, and there had to be something in it for him." Miroslava turned away from Togym, reached into a pocket of her tunic, and pulled out a small piece of gold. She watched Bey Nazar's cousin, Aidar as she said, "This is the very important thing that made Ivan change the map."

Aidar Karimov looked just as confused as Togym had. It was possible that they were both just that good at hiding their expressions, but Vasilii was fairly good at reading people and he didn't think so. Why was Miroslava eliminating suspects? And starting with the best suspects?

Vasilii remembered the famous Holmes quote, the one he'd taught her. "Once you eliminate the impossible, whatever is left, however improbable, must be the truth." Miroslava had looked at him, tilted her head, and asked, "What if two things are left? Or three, or ten?" Vasilii hadn't had an answer. Still didn't. And here Miroslava was busily eliminating suspects. *Why?*

"For a thing to be important, someone has to know about it." Miroslava pocketed the gold and pulled Ivan's notepad out of another pocket. "Ivan knew about that little piece of gold and the probably very large seam of gold that it came from, because he found it in his surveying. He knew the atomic number for gold because of his studies at the Ufa Dacha, and that was what he used. 79. Gold's atomic number. But he also used Greek numbers. I think he meant it as a code though I can't be sure of that, but whether he did or not, it had me stymied. Until I asked Jaroslav what the Greek letters meant, and he told me they were numbers."

She flipped up the pages of the notebook until she got to a specific page. "On June 18, Ivan found the gold nugget on the land of Sultan Aidar. But that didn't do him any good. The land belonged to Sultan Aidar and his clan. And so did the gold." She put the notebook back in her pocket. "But if the railroad went close enough to the gold mine, the railroad would own the land and the gold."

By now the eyes of the nobles and clansfolk in the clearing were darting between Miroslava and Sultan Aidar, and Sultan Aidar was starting to look deeply offended and a bit nervous, which made him look guilty as heck.

Vasilii wasn't buying it. He'd seen the confusion on Sultan Aidar's face when Miroslava held up the gold. Struck by a thought, he looked at Bey Nazar. The smile was gone from his face, and he was looking daggers at Miroslava. That expression was when Vasilii started getting really scared.

"But Ivan didn't own the rail line either. Or so I thought, but Czar Mikhail is strapped for cash. And as I understand it, so is the khan. So payment for people doing important work for the railroad is being made in railroad stock." Miroslava shook her head. "It wasn't enough. Not enough for Ivan to make a false map.

"Czar Mikhail is very rich, but what with running a country and fielding an army he often finds himself short of cash," Miroslava said, and Vasilii—along with everyone else—wondered what that had to do with Ivan falsifying a map. "So when this railroad came up, he didn't have the cash to spare to just buy the land and build the railroad. Instead, he sold stock in the company and paid many of the people involved in the railroad with stock. He paid Vasilii in stock.

He . . . well, he and Salqam-Jangir Khan bought the land that the railroad would go over with stock and, most important from our point of view, he paid Ivan in railroad stock."

Miroslava shook her head again. "It still wasn't enough. Yes, if the railroad owned the land the gold mine was on, it would certainly help, but unless it's a truly huge gold mine it wouldn't make that much difference. It didn't make that much sense, but then I got a telegram from Brandy Bates, now Princess Brandy Gorchakov. I sent her a telegram because she has been heavily involved in the business of the Russian consulate in Grantville, so she knows a great deal about this stuff."

Now Miroslava stopped and looked at Salqam-Jangir Khan, Sultan Togym, Sultan Aidar, Bey Nazar and then generally around the gathering. "And because Brandy, like me, used to work in a bar.

"Anyway, Brandy told me about something called pump and dump. It happened a lot up-time and it happens in Grantville and Magdeburg as well. Also Amsterdam, Brussels, Venice and Genoa. And if they can do it, so can we. In pump and dump, you buy stock, then you make an announcement that makes the stock seem to be worth a lot. People rush to buy the stock, the price goes up, and you sell it before it goes back down. It's called pump and dump because you pump up the stock price before you dump your stock. Aside from the stock that Ivan got paid with, he'd bought even more in the last couple of weeks of his life over the telegraph. That explains why Ivan needed the railroad to go close to the gold mine. But it doesn't explain why he was killed.

"Remember, something becomes important only if you know about it. That gold had been sitting in the ground for thousands of years and as long as no one knew about it, it didn't matter at all. When Ivan found it, it became important to him, but not to anyone else. For it to be a motive in his murder, someone had to know about it." She looked at Bey Nazar as she said that last.

Then everything went to hell.

* * *

Nazar looked at the witch and knew she knew. She had to be a witch. No *woman* could just figure all that out. And if she'd figured out that much, she had figured out the rest. He looked at her then he looked at Jangir, his boyhood friend who had betrayed the Kazakh people to secure his place. Who would now have Nazar executed just to placate the Russian czar. Because the Russian witch had figured out what no one should have been able to figure out. He looked at that old bastard Togym, always so cautious, no guts, not a real man at all. Just a clever schemer, but not as clever as Nazar. It would have worked if it weren't for the witch. He would have been broken using his own tools.

There were three people that Nazar needed to kill before he went down. The witch, Togym, and Jangir. But he was a warrior. He knew he would only get one. The decision in that frozen moment was no decision at all. The witch, in her way, was honorable. Togym was just a bureaucrat. Jangir was the traitor. "Witch!" he shouted, but as he drew his sword, he leapt, not at the witch, but at the boyhood friend who had betrayed everything they stood for. He leapt at Salqam-Jangir Khan.

* * *

Miroslava had been expecting Nazar's reaction, except for one thing. She was expecting him to attack her. Her pistol was loose in its shoulder holster for just that reason. She drew as he leapt, but had to shift her aim because the idiot was going the wrong way.

* * *

Vasilii wasn't sure who was going to attack Miroslava, but he was very intent that they should fail. He too had his pistol ready. He too was thrown off his game by the fact that Nazar wasn't attacking Miroslava but the khan.

* * *

Salqam-Jangir Khan was a smart kid who grew up in an incredibly tough world. This wasn't the first time someone had tried to kill him. And he wasn't even slowed much by the fact that it was a childhood friend. It was simply that the PPK given to him by Czar Mikhail the day after he signed the Constitution of the USSR was still not that familiar to him. He'd fired it, of course, but its bullets were pricey. So he didn't fire it every day.

A MISSION FOR THE CZAR

No one would ever know which bullet hit Bey Nazar first. Well, no one but Miroslava, and she wasn't saying. But he was hit seven times out of twelve shots fired. Fortunately, no one else was hit. At least three of the shots were fatal, possibly four. Given the lack of a top flight surgeon, almost certainly four.

* * *

As the three smoking guns were put away, the whole assembly stood frozen in shock. Then Salqam-Jangir Khan looked at Miroslava. "Why?"

"Because he knew about the gold mine. Bey Nazar had spies planted on us all as soon as we came into his clan territory. His spy on Ivan discovered the gold. She knew it wasn't there, then that it was. So she knew that he hadn't brought it with him. Knowing the date it arrived and having access to the colonel's notebook told them, at least roughly, where to look."

"I got that part, but why attack *me?*" Salqam-Jangir Khan asked. "He was a friend."

"I can tell you that, Salqam-Jangir Khan," said Sultan Aidar. looking down at his cousin with sadness. "Because you betrayed us. The clan chiefs, the sultans, and nobles in your realm. You got 'security,' for whatever that's worth. The peasants, even slaves, got the vote, for whatever *that's* worth. But your nobles, your friends, your class? What did we get? You betrayed us all in Ufa!"

There was a rumble of agreement from the assembled nobility.

And there it is, Vasilii thought. The thing that Czar Mikhail was afraid of. Stated more bluntly than Vasilii was expecting, but in the open at last. The addition of the federal government must inevitably reduce the power of the state nobility. And the khan was young, young enough, perhaps, to say something stupid.

"You get a state constitution as soon as you and the khan write it," Vasilii said.

"What?" Salqam-Jangir Khan asked.

"That was the deal Czar Mikhail made in Ufa. He gave up his theoretically absolute power and got a more stable government of laws. And, in a way, it's the deal you made as well. Give these men, ah, people, a say in how the state laws are made."

That elicited shocked silence, then a somewhat muted level of agreement.

"Have your own Constitutional Convention," Vasilii continued.

CHAPTER 7: CONSTITUTIONAL CONVENTION

Location: Camp East of Druzhba
Date: July 13, 1637

Salqam-Jangir Khan looked at the map. It was a conglomeration of up-time maps of the world that had been in Grantville at the time of the Ring of Fire, cartography done by Russians, mostly the late unlamented Ivan Smirnov, and Kazakh maps which, while artistic and descriptive of the terrain and even quite accurate in their way, were not accurate in terms of number of meters from point a to point b.

However, when you put them all together, you got something that was useful, if still in need of refinement. A straight shot from Ufa to the Kazakh capital of Shavgar would take a single rider on a good horse or a small group of horsemen with spare horses about twenty days, figuring an average of fifty miles a day for such a small well equipped group. For a large force, twice that, and for herders with their herds, a good two months. A steam train on a single track traveling an average of ten miles an hour, including stops, would make the trip in four days. Salqam-Jangir Khan *really* wanted a railroad.

From their present location it would take a small group on horseback about fourteen to sixteen days. Add in wagons and it was going to take a month or more, and that didn't include the time it would take to map the railroad. Especially since the present plan was to head to the Aral Sea then travel by river the rest of the way. There weren't any steamboats on the Syr Darya, not yet.

Meanwhile, Salqam-Jangir Khan had a problem. He needed to have a constitutional convention, and he needed to do it now. He also realized that he needed Vasilii for the convention. He'd attended the one in Ufa, but aside from short visits from his cousin Togym, he was the only Kazakh who had. And he had a bias that would make his nobles question any position he took.

"All right," he muttered to himself, "we'll have the convention on the road. That's more suitable for the Kazakh people anyway." He sent out riders, instructing his nobles to send representatives or come themselves, and to have the peasants and even slaves send representatives as well.

Location: Camp South of Druzhba
Date: July 14, 1637

The new site was almost fifteen miles south of the old. It had taken them half of yesterday and most of today to make the trip and while there were hills in the distance, the ground was as flat as a pancake all the way around the compass. Flat to the north, the east, the south, the west, and all points of the compass in between. It was covered in grass and the herds were making good use of it.

The surveyors were out mapping the route of the rail line and for right now at least, that line was probably going to go straight as an arrow for at least the next thirty miles and more. That was good news because, according to Vasilii's calculations, over ground like this going straight the tractor could pull a train of twenty small wagons or three of the massive *khibitkha* at a speed of thirty miles an hour or better, assuming a worked road bed and most of the weight on a wooden rail. A few hundred mile stretches like this and they would seriously cut the time it took to reach the river.

That was the good news.

Miroslava, after the shoot out at the barbeque, hadn't given him her contract and while they were still sleeping in the same bed, they weren't, ah, "sleeping together," as it were. Miroslava was getting more irritable every day.

And they were going to have to stay here on the road, because the khan and the czar both wanted him here for the Kazakh constitutional convention.

There was a knock on the door of the *khibitkha* and one of the streltzi escorts stuck his head in. "You're wanted at the khan's yurt."

The khan had a *khibitkha*, but *khibitkha* were slow and the khan had ridden fast to get here, so for now he was using a regular yurt, which was a cross between a house and a tent, in that it could be taken down, carted to where it was wanted, and set up again.

Vasilii left without saying goodbye to Miroslava. Maybe he was getting irritable too.

* * *

Rayana asked, "Why are you acting like that?" She was still with them in spite of the fact that Bey Nazar had been her patron and owner. For a while yesterday, it was an even chance whether she and the spy he had placed on Colonel Smirnov would be executed for their complicity in the plot. But Miroslava had pointed out that as slaves they had no choice, which had quite possibly saved their lives. Salqam-Jangir Khan had given them to the Russian mission. Vasilii had freed them and offered them jobs, which had had the effect of turning Rayana from a somewhat taciturn lady into something of a chatterbox. Perfectly willing to share her opinion on everything whether she knew anything about it or not. Not everyone was reacting to their manumission the way Miroslava did.

"Like what?" Miroslava asked.

"Why aren't you fucking Vasilii? Why are you being so mean to him?"

"He doesn't own my contract and I am not being . . ." She was being mean to him, not on purpose, but she didn't know how to stop.

"So you never really liked him?"

Miroslava blinked. "Liked him? What does that have to do with having sex with him?" Miroslava knew that other people saw things differently. Even the other girls at the Happy Bottom had had customers they liked and customers they didn't, and were much more willing to have sex with the ones they liked. And it was even true that Miroslava enjoyed sex with some customers more than she did with others.

But Miroslava was a person of rules. It was all she had to keep the chaos at bay. If someone owned your contract, you had sex with them. Or, as in the case of Madam Drozdov, whoever they told you to have sex with. You didn't have sex with someone just to do it. That was as likely to get you beaten as refusing to have sex if you were told to.

It did occur to Miroslava that since she owned her contract, she could tell herself to have sex with Vasilii, and that was tempting. But it didn't feel right. Miroslava wasn't a bar girl any more, and in her world you had sex if you were married or if it was your job, and that was it.

She tried to explain that to Rayana and was fairly sure from the woman's expression that she was making a hash of it.

"So marry him!"

"Vasilii is very rich and in the upper nobility. He can't marry a bar girl, not even a former bar girl."

"Didn't you say that Brandy Bates Gorchakov was a bar girl?"

That stopped Miroslava, but there were differences. Brandy worked in a bar, but she didn't take off her clothes and she didn't have sex. So she was a bar girl, but only sort of. Brandy was also willing to have children, and Miroslava wasn't.

But . . . maybe?

No.

Vasilii needed an heir. And there weren't any other Lyapunovs anymore. The Sheremetev clan had made a pretty clean sweep. At least, that was the word Vasilii had out of Moscow. Vasilii would have to marry some daughter of a great house, possibly a Cherakasky, since the Cherakasky were the primary patrons of the Lyapunov clan. Miroslava didn't like that idea much because a Cherakasky wife would probably insist that he sever ties with her since by now their relationship was more than just public. It was almost famous.

Vasilii was irritated. Mostly with the situation, but partly with Miroslava. He understood, or at least tried to understand, her situation and her way of looking at the world, but he didn't always like the results. And the recent results were making him wonder if she had ever liked him at all. That hurt. He had believed that she cared for him, that they'd been having sex as much because she wanted to as because he wanted to. But now it felt like she'd only ever had sex with him because he owned her contract and because she assumed that being male that was what he wanted from her. And that made him feel guilty about having sex with her at all. He was also as frustrated by the sudden cessation of sex as Miroslava, and resentful about it.

* * *

Those thoughts took him to the door of the khan's yurt, where he spent the next several hours going over how you organized a constitutional convention in the middle of a slow moving village in transit from Ufa to Alty-Kuduk at the Aral Sea. Not in the yurt, but out in front of the yurt. On what was still a grass-covered field, on folding chairs built by Kazakh craftspeople from up-time designs delivered by way of Moscow and Ufa. Pinned to the side of the yurt was a map of the route of the rail line so far, and it included Alty-Kuduk.

Alty-Kuduk was a fishing village and at their present rate of travel would take them months to reach. On the other hand, it was likely that a railroad to the Aral Sea would mean that Ufa would be well supplied with large freshwater fish and caviar, since the Aral was a freshwater sea.

In spite of his frustration, Vasilii was a problem solver, and especially with the engineers of the Dacha, they learned to examine things in a way most people didn't. Vasilii knew how to do that in other places besides steam engines. So he sat down in a folding chair made of pine and wool felt, and joined the discussion as they mapped out how the convention would be organized, who would attend and vote on the structure of the state government. There were several clan chiefs seated in a rough circle with Salqam-Jangir Khan seated in a camp chair that was a bit more ornate than the others, but no bigger.

"You need a distinction between state government and clan government, and state law needs to supersede clan law. And the rights of a subject of your state need to be the same, whether they are a clan chief or a slave," Vasilii said, after listening to a clan chief he didn't know try to treat his clan custom as federal law for the USSR.

Slavery, it turned out, wasn't as common among the Kazakhs as it had seemed in Ufa when Salqam-Jangir Khan had been the effective leader of the pro-slavery faction. Partly that was because while slaves weren't as common in Kazakh as Vasilii thought, they did provide certain vital skills. It was also because they had just come off of what was supposed to be the biggest slave raid in the last fifty years. Hundreds of skilled slaves, as well as the rifles that Sheremetev had promised them, and they figured they needed those slaves to industrialize. The slaves were also concentrated in the cities and towns. It turned out that slaves were a smaller percentage of the population than Vasilii had thought. However, the Kazakhs did deal in slaves—as in capture them and sell them in China and elsewhere. Nor was there anything in the USSR constitution that would prevent them from continuing to do so. And there was a good chance that should the federal government try to make a law against it, that law would be struck down on the basis of the rights of sovereign states within the union.

So Vasilii found himself trying to convince the khan that rapid industrialization was better than slave-ication of the Kazakh state. Which it was in the long run, but in the short run, slaves would be faster and cheaper. Which the khan, Sultan Togym, and three others of the khan's close associates were quick to point out.

"But you can't get your slaves from raiding other states in the USSR."

96

"No, but we can get them from Russian states that haven't joined the USSR yet."

"Not if it's going to get the czar into a war," Vasilii said. "Remember, foreign policy is the purview of the federal government, not the states."

"You gave up too much, Salqam-Jangir Khan," said one of those advisers. "You gave up things that weren't yours to give. My clan doesn't need the czar's permission to raid. We don't need yours either."

"You do if you expect him to come to your aid when the enemies you made in your raiding retaliate. In fact, you do if you want him to refrain from raiding your villages and taking your wives and daughters as slaves," Vasilii pointed out.

"Such a raid would be quite costly," growled the clan chief.

"A one time expense." Vasilii shrugged. "Then your clan would be gone. Your lands and herds given to other, more reasonable, clans."

"So it's this now. The czar's man speaks for the khan. Doesn't even use the khan to deliver his threats. I thought it would take longer for Mikhail to put off his fig leaf. He's supposed to be shy, after all."

"I wasn't speaking for the khan or delivering threats. I was simply pointing out the logic of the situation," Vasilii said before the khan could say anything. "For that matter, I wasn't speaking for Czar Mikhail. And I'm not speaking for him when I say he's not timid or particularly shy. People, if they have any brains, respond to their situation. A smart man doesn't step on a tiger's tail if he can avoid it.

And Czar Mikhail grew up in a room full of tigers. Big hungry ones whose sole reason for not taking a bite at the imperial crown was the threat of the other tigers."

"And rather than making himself into a tiger, he ran away," the clan chief said.

"Ahh." Vasilii waved at the clan chief. "Here we have the very definition of a fool. For what else do you call a man who would choose to be ruled by a tiger?"

"You dare!" The clan chief leapt up, grabbing the hilt of his sword. Vasilii didn't get up, but his hand did go into his tunic.

"*Stop!*" roared Salqam-Jangir Khan. "Vasilii, do you enjoy shooting holes in my nobles? I thought you were supposed to be a diplomat!" He turned to face the clan chief. "Arman, don't be an idiot. I've seen Vasilii draw. You'd be dead before the sword was half out of its sheath."

Vasilii shrugged, hand still in his tunic. After all, Sultan Arman Nabiyev still had his hand on the hilt of his sword. "Sometimes, Salqam-Jangir Khan, diplomats have to tell the truth, even if the people across from them don't want to hear it." Then, almost as an afterthought, he added, "And I'm not a diplomat. I'm an engineer. I make steam engines, not polite small-talk."

"Craftsman," Arman Nabiyev said in disgust. "He shouldn't be in the councils of the brave at all."

"I quite agree. I have better things to do," Vasilii said. "But Czar Mikhail doesn't want the state of Kazakh to devolve into a bunch of warring clans to be gobbled up by the Zunghar Khanate. So I'm stuck here when I should be working on a flying machine."

"Lies! No one can fly, not even the fabled up-timers."

Vasilii blinked. A few years ago, he would have said the same thing. Before the Ring of Fire, even right after it. But he'd seen the test bed float into the air. He'd seen the *Czarina Evdokia* and the *Prince Alexi*, even the *Princess Anna.* and he'd seen the glider experiments in Ufa, in preparation for the steam powered airplane he was working on—or had been—before he was dragged out here to the hinterlands. He took a breath. He was clearly more upset by the situation with Miroslava than he'd thought.

He turned to the khan and bowed. "I'm sorry, Salqam-Jangir Khan. I shouldn't have spoken so bluntly." He turned back to Arman. "Sultan Arman, I have seen men fly in balloons. I have seen men fly in gliders. I swear before God that this is true. If it was up to me, I would be back in Ufa working with the craftsmen there to make a . . ."

Vasilii paused because he'd run out of words. They were speaking Russian because Vasilii's Kazakh wasn't great and most of the upper level Kazakhs included Russian as well as Chinese in the languages they spoke. The Kazakhs were almost as much traders as they were herders of cattle and sheep. However, they didn't as a rule speak post up-timer Russian, which had several borrowed words from up-timer English and German, and more than a few words with changed meanings. In the field of steam, and to avoid confusion, "power plant" was an adopted English word, not Russian. Political power was Russian. Muscle power was Russian. Steam power was English with a Russian accent. So was electrical power, battery power. He used the English, "steam power plant to run the engines to push the plane through the air. In my frustration at not being able to do my proper job, I spoke more bluntly than I should have."

Again Vasilii paused, but this time for emphasis. "What I said was true, but I should have phrased it more adroitly." *Well,* Vasilii thought, *that sounds better than "I bit your head off because I'm not getting laid."*

✳ ✳ ✳

Sultan Arman Nabiyev looked at the Russian. He'd seen the gunfight and as unhappy as he was with the present situation, given a moment to catch his breath, he realized just how close he'd been to ending up like Bey Nazar. Truthfully, that was part of the reason he was so upset. The idea of being afraid of a craftsman offended him to his very core. But Vasilii Lyapunov said he'd seen men fly. Swore it by his God. And while all Christians were liars, he didn't think Lyapunov was lying about this. If this man really could make devices that let men fly, craftsman was too small a word for what he was. Wizard was closer, but wizards weren't real. Perhaps he now had a definition for "engineer."

He took his own breath and said, "I accept your apology. And I too wish you were back in Ufa making 'pow ur pl a nts.' "

"I don't," Salqam-Jangir Khan said calmly. "Vasilii makes less of himself when he says he's an engineer. He is, but that isn't all he is. He fought on the walls at Ufa and was in the constitutional convention. He is a warrior, statesman and engineer all in one, even if he would put the last first. Accept your fate, Vasilii. We have a state to build here, and we need your skill for that. Build your airships later."

Then they got down to business.

Gorg Huff & Paula Goodlette

CHAPTER 8: A PROPOSAL AND A MURDER

Location: Camp South of Druzhba
Date: July 14, 1637

Vasilii got back to the rolling yurt late that evening to find Miroslava apparently asleep.

Rayana waved him out of the yurt and Vasilii went. He wasn't in the mood for Rayana's advice, but he was even less in the mood to lay down back to back with Miroslava for another night of celibacy.

Almost as soon as they exited the yurt, Rayana said, "You should marry her."

Vasilii blinked. He'd never thought of that. Mostly because Vasilii had never thought that his marriage was something that he would have much say in. He'd known from his early childhood that any marriage would be arranged by his family for political and economic reasons, and would have little to nothing to do with any preferences on his part. In Vasilii's world you didn't marry for love. You married for political or financial advantage and someone with the right *mestnichestvo*. And Miroslava, for all her attributes, didn't offer either of those things.

Or did she?

She was the czar's Holmes. That gave her some rank. The czar had given her some political rank when he gave her a name, and a bit more when he licensed her as a private detective. And the Ufa cops paid her for her consultations.

For that matter, when the khan bought her contract and gave it to her, he'd also given her a license, giving her as much rank in the Kazakh Khanate as in Ufa. Perhaps a bit more. Neither of those, nor both of them together, put her in Vasilii's rank strata. He was the bottom end of the upper nobility, not like Vladimir Gorchakov or Sheremetev. Not like the Cherakasky, but with all the deaths in his family, not that far below them.

Then he stopped and considered a thought. There was political advantage here. Not so much for the Lyapunov family, but for the USSR. Russia, before the Ring of Fire, was as stratified a society as existed in Europe. He knew that Bernie and Natasha wanted to do away with that stratification. He knew that the czar was less enamored of equality before the law, but was willing enough to go along with it. Vasilii tended to agree with Bernie and Natasha, all the more since he'd met Miroslava.

He didn't like what the fact that she was the child of peasants had done to her. He didn't like the way it limited her options. Granted, some of that was poverty. But some of it was the rules that were in place in Russia that made the rank of your family, the rank you were born into, determine everything about you.

If he married her, it would be a challenge to that tradition. Not as much as Natasha marrying Bernie or Vladimir marrying Brandy. It would be another chip away at the structure of law and custom that said Miroslava could be his plaything, even his love, but never his wife. That her children could never inherit his rank.

Almost, he turned and went into the yurt to tell her they were getting married. Then he remembered that she hadn't had sex with him since the khan gave her her contract. What if she didn't want to marry him? That wasn't something he wanted to find out.

He didn't know what to do.

Meanwhile, the moving town was getting bigger and moving again.

Location: Camp farther South of Druzhba
Date: July 16, 1637

The land was getting hilly again. Nothing all that high, but rough terrain that would need bridges and cuts, or rerouting of the railroad to keep the grade from becoming too steep. And the camp, made up of dozens of yurts and at least three of the huge mobile yurts, now had a population of over a thousand people.

Even when on the move, Vasilii was finding himself in wagons, talking to the various sultans and beys of the khan's court about the upper house and whether they should be seated in it or appoint the representative of their clan. And how to let their people vote on the representative to the lower house.

* * *

That night as camp was being set up, Vasilii finally got up the nerve to ask Miroslava about marrying him. He didn't ask her to marry him. He wasn't quite willing to straight up ask her, so instead he said, "What do you think about the idea of us getting married?"

It wasn't very romantic, but Miroslava wasn't actually much more comfortable with romance than Vasilii was.

Miroslava, being Miroslava, considered the question, then said, "I see several problems."

"What problems?"

"A child of mine might be like me."

"I don't see a problem with that," Vasilii said, and it was at least partly true.

Miroslava was silent for several seconds while she worked out what to say. "You don't know what being me is like from the inside. It isn't good. Not comfortable, not safe, not happy. I see everything, hear everything, remember everything, and it's all there, all the time, hard to sort out. It *hurts* to be me. Well, a lot of the time. Most of the time even, it hurts. There are things I like. Things that make me feel good, but there are more things that make me confused and afraid."

"What makes you feel good?" Vasilii asked. He'd known that Miroslava was different and not comfortable with social situations for as long as he'd known her, but he hadn't realized that the cacophony of sensory input was actually painful to her. But he knew Miroslava's nature well enough to understand that she wasn't being figurative. That if she said hurt, she *meant* hurt. And he was looking for something that could make that pain go away, or at least distract from it.

"Sex, solving a puzzle, not so much having solved a puzzle. That's satisfying, but what feels good is solving the puzzle." She listed several foods that she liked, because she could focus on the flavor and push the rest of the world away for a little. And several specific forms of sex. "Cuddling, sometimes. Handling my things back at the Dacha, and reading books."

Well, apparently the lack of sex since she got her contract wasn't because she didn't like sex. "If you like sex, why haven't we been having sex? Is it me you don't like having sex with me?"

"You don't own my contract. You're all right at sex. You're learning. Adequate."

Well, it was apparent that Vasilii wasn't Miroslava's dream lover. "Adequate" wasn't a ringing endorsement. On the other hand, if she'd found him objectionable, she'd have said so. Since he didn't own her contract.

And that was why they weren't having sex. He didn't own her contract. "Miroslava, people have sex without contracts," he blurted, knowing even as he said it that wasn't correct in the case of Miroslava. She was a person of rules, of defined situations. And suddenly he got something that had been buzzing around in the back of his mind since they'd met. She needed the rules to stave off the cacophony of possibilities. Without the rules, there would be too many options, a cacophony of options like the cacophony of sensation that constantly bombarded her.

"That is a good reason to get married. It would provide structure, rules."

"But you need heirs," Miroslava said.

"I'm sure there's a cousin, or second cousin, or even third cousin still around somewhere. Or we can talk to Czar Mikhail and see what he wants to do. He might want the Lyapunov lands to revert to the nation when I pass away."

Miroslava wasn't satisfied with that answer, but for now they let it pass.

They sent a message back to the czar, asking if he would object to the marriage. Vasilii, because of the large number of deaths in his family and in the Cherakasky family that were their patrons, had an important role in the *mestnichestvo* structure. *Mestnichestvo* was designed to keep the great houses great and the lesser houses lesser. A place for everyone and everyone in their proper place. And never allow "your" family to rise above "mine." So, by its nature, *mestnichestvo* didn't respond well to change, and the decimation of the nobility over the past couple of years had rivaled that of the Time of Troubles and the Three Dimitris.

Mikhail was trying to keep the system from shattering because the nobles of the great houses and even of the lesser houses were—as Bernie had stated several times—"going to go batshit crazy" if they lost their *mestnichestvo*. They were as afraid of options as Miroslava was.

Location: Ufa Kremlin
Date: July 17, 1637

Count Lukyan Brezhnev read the radio telegraph message that he had just been handed.

Wish to marry Miroslava Holmes but do not wish to cause you problems. Miroslava doesn't want to have children. I understand her reasons and agree.

It had a note from Czar Mikhail attached.

Lukyan, find a way to do this that won't drive the conservative nobles back to Sheremetev.

Count Lukyan Brezhnev was the protocol officer of the czar's court in Ufa. Contrary to stereotype, he wasn't a fussy little man, clean shaven, and impeccably dressed. He was a fussy big man with a full beard. He wore a sword and knew how to use it.

But he was impeccably dressed, in the Ufa style. He was wearing a bright green silk tunic with shiny brass zippers up the front and on all four pockets. And he kept the family book for the Ufa Kremlin. It was a thankless job, but in his way he loved it. He also owned a print shop that printed things like wedding invitations.

Lukyan was the man who decided who sat where at a royal dinner. He could be overridden by the czar or czarina, but by no one else.

The sword—and his ability to use it—was his response to those who might try to gainsay him.

Oddly enough, Lukyan liked Bernie and Natasha, and positively doted on Anya, because for all his fussiness and attention to detail, he was a very smart man with a deep and profound understanding of Russian history and politics. That was why he was here in this office made of logs in the Ufa Kremlin, not back in Moscow. Because he saw the writing on the wall sooner than most.

Lovely, he thought and smiled. The Cherakasky family had been decimated and the Lyapunovs effectively destroyed in the pogroms Sheremetev had launched right after Czar Mikhail had escaped from the hunting lodge. Vasilii would have died too, if he hadn't been at the Gorchakov Dacha and on the first boat out.

There was, however, a fourteen-year-old girl, Alla Lyapunov, who was living in hiding in Moscow with the Petrov family. Alla—or her part of the family—actually outranked Vasilii by quite a lot. That, in part, was why she was still hiding in Moscow, not here in Ufa. Her branch of the Lyapunov family had been much more conservative than Vasilii's and she wasn't sure of her welcome if she showed up and tried to displace Vasilii.

But now the solution was perfect. Vasilii and the Holmes would adopt the young girl and she would become their eldest daughter as well as keeping his prior family connection. That would indicate that while the internal family politics of the Lyapunov family might be worthy of disapproval, it was at least respecting the outer workings. They wouldn't be trying to foist the daughter of a whore into Moscow high society.

He set the telegram and the note on the blotter of his desk and pulled a sheet of good grade rag paper from the paper shelf in his desk, dipped a steel tip quill pen in the inkwell and began to write. After the salutations and rank he started on the body of the letter.

I think that I have a solution to the Lyapunov situation. My sources indicate that Alla Lyapunov survives and is living as a servant in the house of an acquaintance of Iosif Borisovich Petrov.

Long ago Lukyan had learned that the way to keep a secret was to not tell anyone. Nothing he wrote was a lie. Iosif Borisovich was acquainted with his cousin Georgy Petrov. He dipped his pen again and continued

If you approve, I will approach Iosif Borisovich and together we may contrive to bring the young woman to Ufa, where she may, with their agreement, be adopted by Vasilii and Miroslava with contracts in place so that she will inherit the family properties when they pass from this vale of tears.

Your obedient servant,
Count Lukyan Brezhnev

* * *

Czar Mikhail read the letter, noting in passing as he often did the fine calligraphy that Lukyan always used. If Vasilii and Miroslava agreed, this would be an excellent solution politically. Czar Mikhail didn't remember the girl, but then he hadn't known Vasilii before the Constitutional Convention either.

He turned to his secretary. "Telegraph Vasilii, in code mind you, and ask him if he would be willing to adopt Alla Lyapunov. Oh, and send for Iosif Petrov. He's been keeping secrets again."

The secretary grinned. "Isn't that his job, Your Majesty?"

"Yes, but I want to know how Lukyan found out before me."

* * *

Fifteen minutes later, Iosif showed up, looked at the letter and said, "How the hell did he find out about that?"

"I take it you knew."

"Yes, Your Majesty. Papa told me months ago. When the convention was going on. Because by then the situation had gotten delicate, as well as dangerous."

"Delicate?"

"Vasilii is a signer," Iosif said, and the czar immediately understood. There were two sorts of signers of the Constitution. One was attendees of the convention who were given the option of signing. The others were the representatives of the states. Salqam-Jangir Khan was both and had actually signed the document twice.

But all the people who signed it, the attendees like Vasilii Lyapunov and Vera Ruzukov and others, automatically had their *mestnichestvo* jumped up several pegs. Like the signers of the American constitution had. It didn't make you into a boyar, but prestige attached.

At least, it attached in Ufa.

Back in Moscow, being a signer had somewhat the opposite effect.

Which meant that if Alla Lyapunov showed up, she would, by Moscow standards, outrank her cousin Vasilii, in spite of his being male. But by Ufa standards, she would be outranked by him. Which was a political headache until the situation got resolved.

"Can you get her here?"

"Probably. Right now she is playing the role of a serf in Cousin Georgy's house. The real question is will Vasilii agree to adopt the child? She, by all reports, was a spoiled brat when she arrived on Georgy's doorstep."

Location: Camp farther South of Druzhba
Date: July 17, 1637

The return message was clear. If they were to get married, they should adopt an heir, and Czar Mikhail recommended Vasilii's cousin, Alla Lyapunov.

"I thought she was dead," Vasilii commented. "The last time I saw her she was twelve and a spoiled little monster. Demanding to be allowed to wear makeup. I wonder why Georgy took her in. It can't have been for her personality or her beauty." He shrugged apologetically. "She wasn't all that attractive. Chubby and flat faced."

"Kindness?" Miroslava asked. She didn't know the Petrov family, but from what she'd heard, that family wasn't much given to sentiment. At least not the branch of it that lived in Ufa.

"Possible, but more likely someone thought that a living Lyapunov might be useful at some point. Which was fairly astute."

"Are you sure you want to do this?" Miroslava asked. "I wouldn't inflict my situation on a child, but that doesn't mean you shouldn't have children."

"Yes, I'm sure," Vasilii said, then admitted, "I always thought I would have children and was sort of looking forward to being a father, but I love you."

Miroslava nodded, but at the same time she thought. It was, after all, what Miroslava did. She looked at the situation and concluded that neither marriage nor adoption meant that Vasilii couldn't father other children. But that discussion could wait until she'd had more time to think about it.

Vasilii nodded too and said, "We'll radio the czar and agree to his proposal. We might be able to get her to learn to read at least. The last time we talked, she assumed that anyone who read was probably given to other unnatural urges." He didn't sound enthusiastic about the project.

There was a knock at the door of the yurt.

Vasilii answered and it was Lieutenant Ilya Blinov, the commander of the streltzi guards now that Colonel Smirnov was dead. "The Kazakhs have a dead body they want the Holmes to look at."

* * *

The body was behind a yurt in a spot not easily seen. From tan lines, it had been stripped of at least one ring and probably several others. He was wearing vambraces, steel, but not fancy. They hadn't been taken, which was a good thing because the killer who had stabbed the victim in the gut had gotten blood on his hands and transferred some of that blood from hand to vambrace in the form of two bloody fingerprints, an index and middle finger from the left hand, as well as a smudged thumbprint. That didn't prove the killer was left-handed, but it was suggestive.

The victim was identified. He was Erasyl Iskakov Bey, and he lived in the yurt he was found behind. Erasyl Iskakov was, according to the other people living in the yurt, given to keeping low company. And, in spite of the prohibition, he was a drinker.

Questioning revealed that aside from the ring, he'd been relieved of a purse that contained little gold, but a fair amount of silver, a jeweled brooch on his hat, and a dagger with silver inlays on the handle and a jeweled pommel.

It wasn't until two hours later that they managed to inform the czar that they agreed to his proposal and, if practical, Vasilii's new daughter should be brought to Ufa.

CHAPTER 9: A YEAR AT HARD LABOR

Location: Home of Georgy Petrov
Date: June 28, 1636

Alla Lyapunov crouched in an alley and watched a patrol of dogboys go by and hated the world. She was thirteen years old, five feet three inches tall, with brown hair and eyes. She weighed just under a hundred pounds. She was dressed in a cotton dress, which was quite expensive. Not as much as silk, but much more expensive than wool. She grimaced at the dogboys, showing a small gap between her two front teeth.

"Sheremetev's hounds," they were calling them now, after Czar Mikhail escaped and Alla's world went to hell.

Four hours ago, she'd been playing, well, gossiping, with Irina. Irina's mother came into Irina's room and ordered Alla out of the house, explaining that the Lyapunov clan had been accused of witchcraft because of Cousin Vasilii.

"But Cousin Vasilii works at the Dacha!" Alla had cried.

"It's just an excuse, girl," Irina's mother explained. "It's your whole family. You're tied too closely to the Cherakasky clan, but you're not boyars yourselves."

"Great Uncle Yuri was," Alla said.

"That was sixty years ago, girl."

It struck Alla as strange that Irina's mother hadn't called her by name since she'd come into the room. Always before she called her Alla. But before she could ask about it, she was out the door and told to go home.

She had gone home, but she'd been upset by the whole situation and in no hurry to talk to Mama about it, so she had hidden in the shadows next door to her family's townhouse for over an hour, trying to decide what to do.

Which was why she wasn't in her house when Sheremetev's hounds broke in her family's front door and started killing people.

She hadn't seen it, but she'd heard it. And she'd seen the bodies. They'd dragged them out and laid them in the street. Her mother, father, older brother, and younger brother and sister. All very clearly dead. Her mother with her clothes ripped away.

Alla had hidden in that alley for the whole thing and stayed right there after the dogboys had left. Afraid to go out where people might see her, but unable to leave. Finally, feeling ashamed that she hadn't done anything, she slunk away. And wandered, keeping to shadows.

She couldn't go to her friends. She'd been at a friend's when this started. There was no help there. She thought back, her mind bounding all over the place, looking for anything, and she remembered Father mentioning that Boris Ivanovich Petrov was a spy. The only Petrov she knew even vaguely was Nadia Petrov, who wasn't a friend. Not really of the right social level to be her friend.

But by now she was really hungry.

* * *

Nadia Georgivna Petrov wasn't a fan of Alla Lyapunov, who, in Nadia's opinion, was a spoiled brat. Happy to pull rank at the least excuse. They did attend the same church and the same Sunday school. And normally she'd be more than happy to turn Alla over to any handy adult to be properly punished, but these weren't normal times. Her brother had told her about the Lyapunov purge less than an hour ago, and, well, Alla sent to her room without supper, great. Alla raped and murdered . . . Nadia wasn't quite willing to go that far. She called her brother. He called their mother. She also wasn't willing to turn Alla out, and she brought the girl in and took her to Papa.

* * *

Georgy heard the girl out and, not for the first time, cursed Cousin Boris and his position in the embassy bureau. He, like his wife, wasn't willing to throw a child to Sheremetev's dogs, but he'd be a lot happier if she just left. "If you want to stay here, girl, you will cease to be Alla Lyapunov. Pick a name. You will only need one. Not even a patronym, much less a family name. For you're going to be a serf." He leaned forward over the girl. "I don't mean you'll pretend to be a serf. I mean you *will* be a serf. You'll work like a serf, eat like a serf,

119

and be punished like a serf if you misbehave, which you will because you don't know how to be a proper serf. If that's not acceptable to a high and mighty Lyapunov, the back door is open. Feel free to leave anytime. Do you understand me, girl?"

Clearly terrified, the girl nodded, and Georgy wished she'd gone off in a huff.

Location: Home of Boris Petrov
Date: June 30, 1636

"Have a seat, cousin," Boris said, ushering Georgy to a seat in the small office. "How are things in the streltzi bureau?"

"Things are fine," Georgy said, taking the padded chair. Then he snorted at Boris' raised eyebrow. "Things are disastrous, but not noticeably worse than yesterday. That's not why I'm here."

"Why are you here?" Boris asked, but he didn't go to his desk. Instead he went to one of the new Coleman lamps and pumped it up.

It was already a well lit room with south facing windows glazed in the new mostly flat glass produced by a factory in Moscow from designs provided by the Gorchakov Dacha. Still, it was after nine and the sun was getting ready to set. The shadows covered Boris' desk.

Georgy took a moment to look around the room. It was over a year since he'd been in Boris' house. There was a new filing cabinet in the corner. It had a padlock on it, and, briefly, Georgy wondered what was in it. Then quickly decided he didn't want to know. The truth was Georgy was uncomfortable with his older cousin. He knew that having a cousin in charge of the Grantville desk of the Embassy

Bureau was an advantage, and Boris had provided him with information and equipment that had materially improved his situation in the Streltzi Bureau and on the family lands. But having a spy in the family wasn't quite comfortable for a military man, which was how Georgy thought of himself, even if he was stuck behind a desk for now.

"You were going to tell me why you were here?" Boris asked. Apparently Georgy had been ruminating a bit too long.

"Sorry, Boris. It's a bit delicate. I need some advice."

"It must be if you want advice from me," Boris said.

"You know about the Lyapunov family?"

"Rather more than you do, I suspect. Vasilii Lyapunov got away clean. He's in Ufa with Czar Mikhail, and that makes Sheremetev eliminating the rest of the family worse than useless."

"Vasilii isn't the only one they missed," Georgy blurted.

Boris went still. "Who else?"

"Alla Pavelevna is alive."

"That's the main line," Boris said. "If she were to be found, there would be a quick marriage, an unpleasant honeymoon, and a quick death in her future. At which point, a Sheremetev connection would own the Lyapunov lands and serfs. Which they are claiming they do, since Vasilii is an up-timer trained witch."

"What if she were to escape to Ufa?"

"That's more problematical. Vasilii spent the last five years in the Gorchakov Dacha becoming a steam head and absorbing up-timer attitudes. I suspect that Czar Mikhail is happy enough to have him as *the* Lyapunov. Replacing him with Alla . . . well, she's a young girl. It might well be a case of another quick marriage, though I doubt the short life would follow. Czar Mikhail wouldn't countenance that sort of thing.

"Tell me, Georgy, how did you find out that Alla is alive?"

Georgy told him and finished with, "I don't think I could turn over a teenage girl to Sheremetev."

"That speaks well of your decency, and probably your intelligence. You would be rewarded at first, but then Sheremetev would start to wonder 'why did she come to you?'"

"By the way, why did she come to you?"

"I asked her that. She and Nadia are in the same Sunday school class, but not friends. She'd been turned out of a friend's house, which was probably a good thing. She probably would have been found. She was desperate, so she chose Nadia and hoped."

Boris shrugged. "Given the circumstances, the smartest thing she could have done. And it suggests that she's a good judge of character."

Georgy wished that she'd been a bit less astute, or at least had picked someone else. "You think I should send her to Ufa?"

Boris considered, then shook his head. "Not right now. Everything is confused, but Sheremetev's dog boys are on a rampage. For now, at least, the smart bureaucrat keeps his head down and stays out of politics."

"What about your son?"

"I've disowned him, but I've also informed the new head of the Embassy Bureau that he's in Ufa to keep an eye on Bernie. Which has been his job since he was assigned to the Dacha in the first place."

"And is he reporting on Bernie?" Georgy asked in spite of himself.

Boris smiled a proud paternal smile. "Of course he is, and reporting to him. That boy's going to go far if they don't hang him first."

Georgy shook his head. He didn't understand the mindset of a spy. "What do you think I should do about the girl, Alla?"

"Keep her on as a serf you've brought in from the country. But not too close to your family. Keep her in the kitchen or cleaning chimneys, not as your daughter's personal maid. Nowhere a guest might see her and recognize her."

A "middle class" house in the seventeenth century had servants, usually as many servants as it had family members. They were necessary and didn't leave the family lounging about doing nothing. To keep a house running took all of them, family and servants. One more servant brought in from the family estates to help in the kitchen or back garden wouldn't be a surprise. Especially right now, when so many serfs were running for Ufa.

For that matter, Georgy had lost three serfs from his household and over a dozen from his lands, which was a third of his serfs. Which both shocked and angered him. He treated his serfs well and they should be more loyal.

Location: Home of Georgy Petrov
Date: July 15, 1636

"Anna" used two rags to lift the heavy pot off the hearth fire in the kitchen. She had failed to do that a week ago and had burned her hand rather badly. The chief cook thought she was perhaps the worst, laziest, stupidest pot girl he'd ever seen in his life. A fact he spoke of often when she was nearby.

It was horribly unfair, but everything about her life had been unfair since the dog boys had murdered her family. She put the pot on the table and used tongs to pull the boiled utensils out, and placed them on a cloth to dry. Cook was determined that the slow plague wouldn't hit this house. He'd lost a cousin to it before Bernie Zeppi had shown them what to do. He wasn't going to lose anyone else, even a stupid pot girl, and certainly not the Captain or the family. Hands were washed, utensils were washed, everything was washed in this house, in this kitchen.

That was what she did all day, everyday. While she was pulling the silver forks out of the still boiling water, she was interrupted. The majordomo came in, carrying a bag. "Give me your attention," he said, and most everything stopped. There was a leg of lamb on a spit that still had to be turned, but everything else stopped.

"Miss Nadia has a gift for the lower staff."

Alla, now Anna, hadn't spoken to Nadia since two days after she got here. That was one of the rules. She was never to speak to any of the family unless she was spoken to first. That applied to all the servants, but especially to Anna because no one must suspect that they knew who she was. For their safety and for hers.

The gift was a breviary. And all the kitchen servants got one, not just Anna. But Alla realized that it was the only way that Nadia could give her a breviary. It was a generous gift, since to give her one, Nadia had to give one to everyone in the kitchen. Alla, Anna, wasn't stupid, whatever the cook thought, and she wasn't lazy. She'd just never learned how to do the sort of work that was needed in the kitchen. She was getting better. She was still exhausted every night, but not as exhausted.

Cook thanked the majordomo. "Please thank Miss Nadia for all of us. Let her know that we appreciate her gift." Then he hesitated.

"What is it, Yuri?" asked the majordomo.

"The breviaries are all very nice, but that new cookbook, *The Secrets of Twentieth Century French Cooking*, would help us serve the family better."

"I'm sure it would, Yuri, but Miss Nadia wanted something she could give all the kitchen staff, not just the cook."

Timidly—she did everything timidly these days—Anna half lifted a hand.

The majordomo looked her way, and said, "Yes, girl? You had something to say?"

"Ah, anything from the Dacha? The education books?"

"Can you read, girl?"

"A little, sir."

"How many people here can read?"

Anna and Cook raised their hands, and the cook was hesitant.

"Very well. I will mention the request, and if it's granted you can start teaching the others their letters."

Location: Home of Georgy Petrov
Date: August 3, 1636

"Well, you're getting your cookbook, Yuri," the majordomo announced. "They arranged it through his cousin." He handed a large leatherbound book to the cook. "And here is a basic dictionary. You, girl, the one who can read, I want you to start teaching the other kitchen staff the basics."

* * *

It was almost three hours later that the cook decided that it was time for the staff to start practicing their letters.

The truth was Alla had never been a particularly studious girl, more concerned with games and gossip and boys and makeup than books or prayers. But she did have the basics and the basic dictionary had a lot of pictures in it. Anna learned that teaching someone else something that you only half know is a very good way to learn it, and it was better than carrying heavy pots of water around or scrubbing pots with a wire brush.

Location: Home of Georgy Petrov
Date: August 5, 1636

"Anna!" shouted Cook. "Come over here, you lazy scut."

Anna didn't know what she'd done, but when the cook called in that voice, you didn't hesitate.

He grabbed her by her arm and pulled her into a corner, then he leaned down and whispered, "What's that word?"

The word was in a different print face than the rest of the recipe. It was "Confit" and Anna guessed it was a French word. She turned to the back of the book where there was an index of French terms. It turned out that confit meant to cook more slowly at a lower temperature for a longer time, in grease, oil or sugar water. In this case, the pork belly was to be marinated in a specific marinade and cooked for several hours.

"Will that sterilize the pork belly?" Cook asked. He was a demon on sterilization. Anna didn't know, so the recipe was put aside till they could find out.

This incident started a pattern and Anna would be pulled aside to help the cook read the recipe book. Over the months she got to know the recipes in the French cookbook and as they were added to the family menu, she was often called on, not only by Cook but by the two assistant cooks, to tell them what the recipe for this or that was. She was making a place for herself in the kitchen and could almost forget sometimes that she was not a peasant, but the daughter of a house that once upon a time had ranked high in the family books of *mestnichestvo*.

Life went on like this for three months, then six, with the issues of the wider world not having much effect on her life.

Location: Home of Georgy Petrov
Date: February 27, 1637

Elina waved the broadsheet at Anna. "They sent Bernie Zeppi to negotiate with General Shein."

Anna rolled her eyes. Elina was taking to reading a bit too well for Anna's tastes. Well, she was taking to reading the wrong things. Those broadsheets were silly.

"And the army marched out of Moscow last week," Anna answered. "You know that the Captain was upset he was kept here instead of being put in command of a company of streltzi."

In the kitchen, they always referred to Georgy Petrov as "the Captain," to his wife as "Lady Petrov," and the children as "Miss Nadia," and "Master Gregory," and "young Master Oleg." Young Master Oleg was seven and the terror of the nursery. Master Gregory was attending classes at the Kremlin war college and there was regular speculation on who they would find for Miss Nadia to marry.

At first Alla had found the way the servants gossipped about their "betters" shocking, but Anna, by now, joined in with glee.

But Elina's interest in the Flying Squirrel and his revolutionary pamphlets wasn't harmless gossip. It was radical politics and politics had killed her family. On the other hand, Elina was the second assistant cook and a skilled baker who now provided the family with hot buttered croissants every morning. Anna was in no position to rebuke someone so far above her in the kitchen pecking order. Actually, Anna was afraid that any morning now, she would wake up and Elina would be gone, having run off to Ufa.

That still happened on a fairly regular basis. There was a constant trickle of defections. And the largest part of that trickle came from the servant classes, serfs, and slaves.

By now there were people who made their living hunting down runaways. But that wasn't why Anna hadn't run. Anna hadn't run because Czar Mikhail was going to lose. He lacked the strength to be a real leader like Ivan the Terrible. So her father had said many times, and so she believed. Sheremetev, much as she hated him for what he'd done to her family, didn't lack that strength.

She read through the pamphlet, which didn't actually say that much. Just that Bernie Zeppi had been dispatched to the north to consult with General Shein and Elina wanted to turn that into Shein joining the czar.

Location: Home of Georgy Petrov
Date: March 31, 1637

"The constitutional convention has started in Ufa," Elina crowed. She had another broadsheet.

It was true. The constitutional convention was active in Ufa, and there was even a list of names that she mostly didn't know. Not all of them were famous. She knew about General Izmailov, who was there representing General Shein, but though Shein had sent a delegate, he hadn't committed to join. Then she froze. There it was in black and white.

Lyapunov, Vasilii, representing the Ufa Dacha.

Cousin Vasilii was alive and in Ufa. It made sense. He'd worked and lived at the Gorchakov Dacha back when it was the only one. But it made a hash of the reason for attacking her family. Why murder Papa and Momma, who were about as conservative as any Lyapunov got, and let the radical run off to Ufa?

That night, Anna carefully wrote out a note to Nadia.

Vasilii alive in Ufa. Why kill my parents?

She knew it was breaking the rules, but she had to know.

Location: Home of Georgy Petrov
Date: April 3, 1637

"Anna," Cook said, "take this tray of cheese and biscuits up to Miss Nadia and Master Gregory."

There was also a bottle of tea and glasses.

"You will stay up there and serve them until they release you."

There were a few odd looks at that, but not many. By now people in Moscow had mostly forgotten about the Lyapunov family and most people who remembered thought they were all dead.

* * *

Miss Nadia and Master Gregory were at a table with a tabletop war game between them. Nadia was playing the defender of Ruzuka while Gregory was playing the attacking force of Poles.

Master Gregory waved her toward the table. "Put the tray on the table." Then he got up and went to the door, looked through, then closed it.

"I talked to Cousin Boris after Nadia got your note."

"Cousin Boris?" Anna asked. Then she remembered. The kitchen staff didn't approve of Cousin Boris. The Captain's cousin was in charge of the Grantville desk of the Embassy Bureau. Not a proper soldier like the Captain was and Master Gregory was going to be. Useful fellow, certainly, but not quite proper. All of which she'd learned since becoming a servant in the Captain's house. When she'd been Alla Lyapunov, she'd not known that Nadia had a cousin, much less that he was a high ranked spy.

"Well, Papa's cousin Boris, but he can keep a secret. He's a spy, you know. Before he got put in charge of the Grantville desk, he went to Grantville with Vladimir Gorchakov and he knows half the most important people in the USE personally. Especially the up-timers."

It was obvious to Anna that Gregory was more of a fan of his cousin than his father was. By now she knew that the servants mostly took their cue from the majordomo and the majordomo took his from the Captain.

"Why not ask your father?"

Nadia was shaking her head. "Papa would be angry if he found out you wrote me a letter. He might even turn you out."

"He won't do that," Gregory said. "You're *the* Lyapunov, not your cousin Vasilii. And, especially now, with the Kazakh investing Ufa, you're potentially very valuable.

"If your cousin dies, or Ufa is taken, I don't know what will happen. If the czar is killed, Sheremetev will make a try for the crown, and he's in the best position. But he's not popular.

"For right now, as long as Ufa holds out, you're potentially very valuable to both sides. If you were to go to Ufa, you'd be senior to your cousin. Which is why we're, well, Cousin Boris, isn't sure how welcome you'd be."

"Never mind that," Nadia said. "Tell her what Cousin Boris said about why they went after her family."

"It's about the money," Gregory said. "It always is with the Sheremetev family. Sheremetev could care less about Vasilii's work on steam engines except that he'd like to hire him to work on his. It was your family's lands and the fact that you're a close Cherakasky connection. They wanted your property, and they wanted to weaken the Cherakasky family. They had to go after them after Shermetev killed Dmitri Mamstriukovich Cherakasky. There were other Cherakasky connections, but none as close as yours."

"Mother was a Cherakasky cousin," Alla agreed.

"And Dmitri Mamstriukovich was a powerful man. He was in charge of three bureaus. After killing him, Sheremetev had to make an example to keep the rest in line. Your family was close enough to hurt, but not quite so close as to force them into rebellion. Though Cousin Boris says that what happened to your family was part of what convinced Prince Iakov Kudenetovich Cherakasky to go to Ufa."

"Not that it will do him much good," Alla said. "Papa always said that Mikhail wasn't strong enough to be a real czar."

"Our father says the same thing," Nadia said.

"Not as much anymore," Gregory said, and Alla could tell that Gregory didn't agree that Mikhail was weak. She looked at him in surprise and he sighed. "If they lose at Ufa, it's all over. But they didn't lose. The Kazakhs hit them and they held. They are still holding. Ismailov is there, and if he's not as good as General Lebedev, he is a good general."

Nadia groaned.

Gregory looked at her for a moment, then chose to ignore her. He looked at Alla and said, "General Tim, ah General Lebedev, is holding out fine in Kazan. And by now it's leaked that the plan that saved Rzhev was General Lebedev's, back when he was a brand new lieutenant." He waved at the board game that he and Nadia were playing when Alla came in. It was a painted sheet of the stuff they called cardboard. It had a map of Rzhev and a grid of six sided spaces. On those spaces were small cardboard pieces in different colors with different little shapes drawn on them and next to the cardboard was a set of two dice. "I've played this game hundreds of times and the students in the war college thousands of times. I do pretty well. But General Lebedev did it the first time. The game is based on his defense of Rzhev."

"Papa says it's based on General Izmailov's defense of Rzhev."

"Which would be a good thing for Ufa," Gregory said. "But the word in the war college is that it was Lieutenant Lebedev's plan."

Alla could tell that this was an ongoing argument with Nadia taking their father's side and Gregory taking the part of his fellow students at the war college. To Alla, it seemed unlikely that a boy not much older than Gregory could come up with the plan that saved Rzhev. She did remember gushing over how brave young Lieutenant Lebedev had been moving the guns under General Izmailov's orders. "I'm sure he was very brave moving the guns in the final battle. But that—"

Nadia groaned again. "Don't get him started!"

"What?"

"Those orders," Gregory said. "The ones that General Izmailov gave Lieutenant Lebedev to move the guns. No one knew anything about them until after the battle. And they would have. Why would General Izmailov give secret orders to a lieutenant when he had no idea if he would be in the right place to do anything? If he was going to give those orders, it should have been to every officer under his command. But he *didn't*!" Gregory was leaning forward like he was going to fall on Alla and beat her into agreement.

Alla leaned back, held up her hands in surrender, or at least to indicate he should stay back. And Nadia hit him in the arm. "You're scaring Alla." She looked over at Alla. "Boys! They lack mature judgment, Mama says."

Gregory sat back a little sheepishly, but he said, "It's true anyway. General Lebedev moved the guns on his own."

"Why would General Izmailov lie about it?"

Nadia groaned again.

"It depends on who you ask." He grinned. "Actually, it usually depends on the family rank of who you ask. If they have a lot of rank, they say it's because Izmailov is a glory hound, even though he's never been seen as one before. But if you ask someone with a lower family rank, it's because of *mestnichestvo*. Because they didn't want the precedent that a person acting on their own because they had a high family rank . . ."

As Gregory talked, Alla felt herself wanting to cry in a way she hadn't in months. This was like the discussions that used to bore her to tears at the family dinner table. Papa and Mama arguing over the political situation and family rank. The effect of the Dacha on politics and business in Russia. Whether Russia should attack Poland and try to take Smolensk before the Poles used it to attack Moscow. Whether Shein was a genius or just lucky. She remembered wishing something would catch fire in the kitchen just to get them to shut up about it all.

Now she'd give just about anything to be back there listening to Mama and Papa arguing.

But that would never happen again. Mama and Papa were dead, along with her brothers and sisters. Only "Crazy Cousin Vasilii" was still alive. And he was off in Ufa, where Sheremetev had the czar treed and would pull him down when he got around to it. No one really believed that stuff about Czar Mikhail being under a spell. He just wasn't strong enough to be a real czar.

But wait . . . Gregory was saying . . .

Suddenly she blurted, "Do you really think that Czar Mikhail could win?"

"Papa doesn't," Nadia said quickly.

"No, he doesn't, and six months ago I agreed with him. But six months ago we all thought Czar Mikhail's "boy general" would be dead in a ditch by now. And he's not. It all depends on Ufa. If the czar can hold out in Ufa, he has a shot."

"Papa says it doesn't matter. Even if he holds in Ufa, the army will just bypass Kazan and march to the czar's refuge in Ufa."

"And the czar will get . . ."

"Wait, please!" They kept going over this and over it, just like she and her brothers and sisters had argued.

"Oh, sorry. What is it?" Nadia asked.

"I need to know. Should I go to Ufa?"

They both shut up and looked at each other.

"Not right now. Certainly you'd never get there, with the place under siege by the Kazakhs. If Ufa holds out . . ." Gregory shook his head. "It's like I said before, Cousin Boris isn't sure how welcome you would be in Ufa right now. With Vasilii as *the* Lyapunov, having him represent the Dacha in the constitutional convention, it looks like the czar is respecting *mestnichestvo*. Even like he's gotten the Dacha to respect *mestnichestvo*. Which is helping him with the more conservative families.

"But if you showed up and he left Vasilii in the convention instead of you, that would look like he wasn't respecting it. And if he put you in Vasilii's place, it would look like he was bowing to family rank over everything else. No matter what he did it would offend a bunch of people he doesn't want to offend. Cousin Boris doesn't think that Czar Mikhail would bury your body in a ditch and say you never got there. But he thinks that, for now at least, it's better that Vasilii remain *the* Lyapunov."

"So you're going to have to stay here for a while," Nadia said.

"Also, right now, there is no one to take you there," Gregory added.

They talked a bit more, then Alla disappeared, and Anna took the tray back down to the kitchen.

✳ ✳ ✳

After that, every week or so she would be sent up to "wait on" Nadia. Sometimes Gregory would be there, sometimes not. But Nadia explained that her father must never know.

CHAPTER 10: A MESSAGE FROM KAZAKH

Location: Home of Georgy Petrov
Date: April 14, 1637

On her next trip to "wait on" Nadia, Alla already knew that the czar had made some sort of deal with the Kazakh khan and, for now at least, the khan was sitting in on the convention. His army was still outside Ufa, but it wasn't attacking. And there were rumors that Director-General Sheremetev had survived an assassination attempt. There were also rumors that he hadn't survived, and no one seemed to know where he was.

"You still shouldn't go to Ufa, Papa says," Nadia said as soon as the door was closed. "Vasilii is still the Ufa Dacha's delegate to the convention. And no one knows what's going to happen anyway. It's just a truce, not a peace. But Papa is worried, and Gregory wants to run off to Ufa and join Czar Mikhail. Oh, set the tray on the table and sit down."

After that, they talked. Alla learned that Nadia thought Gregory's friend, Ivan, was dreamy, and that the czarina's new makeup looked good, whatever Mama said.

Location: Home of Georgy Petrov
Date: April 18, 1637

Elina held up the broadsheet and said, "He did it. Czar Mikhail got Salqam-Jangir Khan to agree to the constitution. He signed the USSR constitution."

She handed the broadsheet to Anna, who read the report. It was a long report. And while Salqam-Jangir Khan took pride of place, the name that struck Alla was Vasilii Lyapunov. He signed for the Ufa Dacha. And she realized she still couldn't go to Ufa.

Location: Home of Georgy Petrov
Date: May 3, 1637

Elina was sniffing disapproval. Apparently Czar Mikhail had done something she didn't like.

"What is it?" Cook asked, grinning.

"He's given a whore a name and a title," Elina said. "It was bad enough when he made that blacksmith into gentry, but a whore? And he declared her a private detective. Well, at least he didn't give her lands.

"Apparently, she got her hooks into a noble and the czar did him a favor. It's always the same. I wonder what she did to get the Lyapunov to want her given a name."

"I can guess," said Cook.

Alla could guess too, and she wondered what had gotten into Crazy Cousin Vasilii. This could seriously hurt the family. She froze then. The family . . . the family was dead, except for her and Vasilii.

Location: Home of Georgy Petrov
Date: July 20, 1637

"Come in, Alla," Georgy Petrov said, and took a look at the girl.

A year had made a difference. She was two inches taller at a guess, and thinner. Not the little butterball that had landed on his doorstep a year ago. She wasn't wearing makeup and she was dressed as a kitchen servant in a stained apron over a heavily patched dress. The hair was still brown, as were the eyes, and she still had the gap between her front teeth. But she looked healthy enough.

"We have a letter here. Well, an encrypted telegram from my cousin's son to him, by way of a trusted agent in the telegraph office." Georgy looked over at a short, stocky man with a short beard starting to go gray.

✳ ✳ ✳

Anna hadn't been in this room since she arrived at the Petrov home.

"It's quite real, I assure you, Georgy."

"So you've said, Cousin Boris," Georgy Petrov said.

So this was the famous Cousin Boris, the spy. Somehow Alla had expected someone taller and not quite so chubby. Boris didn't look dashing or sneaky or sly, or anything really. He just looked ordinary, a bureaucrat that you would pass on the street and never notice at all.

He turned to Alla. "Your cousin Vasilii wants to adopt you."

"What?" Anna blurted. It made no sense, and then it did. "Did he get his doxie pregnant?" she asked in disgust. The servants' quarters in the home of Georgy Petrov were rather more socially conservative than Georgy's family and Georgy was more conservative than his Cousin Boris, who was no shining light of liberalism. The motto in the servants' quarters might as well be "a place for everyone and everyone in their place." They didn't approve of people like Miroslava Holmes getting above themselves. They were sort of okay with prostitutes, as long as they *stayed* prostitutes and didn't aspire to positions of respect and honor.

And, to a great extent, Alla had absorbed that attitude from them.

"I have no idea," Cousin Boris said. "It's one possibility and the message didn't go into detail. But, yes, the plan is apparently to combine your and Vasilii's status and so avoid offending propriety by making the child of a bar girl—whatever her other abilities—into the next Lyapunov."

Georgy Petrov snorted at the "other abilities" comment. And Boris shook his head. "Don't scoff, Goergy. From my son's reports, she's tracked down several murderers."

"And let 'Honey Ryder' get away."

Boris started to say something, stopped, took a breath, looked at Georgy, and then at Alla, then back to Georgy. "There is a principle the up-timers express as 'need to know.' It's rather important in my work. And, dear cousin, there is a great deal that you *don't* need to know about Honey Ryder." He looked at Alla. "What you probably *do* need to know, Alla, is about Miroslava Holmes. And you need to know it now before your pre-judgments about her get too firmly set.

"Czar Mikhail didn't give her a last name to please Vasilii Lyapunov. He did it because she was the person who solved the murder of Larisa Karolevna Chernoff's mother and discovered the plot to murder Larisa Karolevna Chernoff while she was still in her mother's womb. Both of which were very useful to the czar and are part of the reason that Sheremetev is still missing."

The Sheremetev faction was still holding on in Moscow, but effectively, no one was in control for most of the length of the Volga. Sort of an armed truce reigned.

"And that's the reason, well, part of the reason, that Georgy and I think you should go to Ufa. With Sheremetev missing and Czar Mikhail safe in Ufa with the Kazakh's securing his southeastern border and in control of the Volga from Kazan south, no one is even trying to stop people with valid papers from traveling. They are still chasing down peasants who run, but not a dvoriane. Which is how you will be traveling. You and Gregory.

"You will be Gregory's sister, and Gregory will be on a mission for his family to buy fish from the Caspian Sea."

Alla wasn't all that sure how she liked the idea of Gregory being her brother. He was altogether too cute to be a brother.

"How will you explain my absence, Father?" Gregory asked.

"You ran off to Ufa with a servant girl," Georgy said. "Nothing political, just an idiot lad, attracted by a skirt. I will, of course, disown you. Oh, and, Gregory, while you are traveling, you will treat Alla as a sister, not a servant girl. Is that clear?"

"Yes, of course, Father," Gregory said, blushing.

He had a cute blush. Alla felt her own face heat.

Location: Steamboat on the Oka River
Date: July 22, 1637

Alla, dressed in Nadia's clothes, stood on the promenade of the two-story steamboat and watched the river go by. The boat was crowded, and it was crowded with people travelling under false papers. And most of them were doing a much worse job of hiding the fact than Alla and Gregory were. Not that anyone was paying any attention to two teenagers. Not when one was armed with a six-shot revolver.

Six years after Bernie Zeppi arrived in Russia to be followed by copies of whole encyclopedias of knowledge, the gun shops of Moscow were in full production. Revolvers were still out of the range of peasants and an expensive luxury for streltzi, but for a deti boyar like Gregory was pretending to be, and Alla really was, or a dvoriane like Gregory was, they were almost a requirement. Gregory had gotten his the day he'd entered the war college at the Moscow Kremlin.

Alla's white makeup proclaimed her to be a member of the nobility, and a conservative one at that. Between those things, the purser who took their money had hardly even looked at their papers.

Not that the papers proclaiming her to be Nadia Vetrov weren't perfect. They were, since they had been made by the official Kremlin printshop. The same shop that made the papers for boyars of the Duma.

Cousin Boris, it turned out, was a very important man these days. And much too vital to the continuing flow of information from Grantville to be removed. Something that Alla hadn't realized until they were on the steamboat. Gregory was worried about his father getting in trouble for his defection, but not about Cousin Boris, whose son ran the Grantville desk in Ufa.

She was jostled by a man who moved on quickly. It wasn't for some minutes that she realized that the ten kopecks of ready money in her purse was gone.

She went back to the room that she and Gregory were sharing with four other people as the steam boat made its way east.

Location: Kazan
Date: July 25, 1637

Alla and Gregory got off the boat at Kazan, where they went directly to the radio telegraph, and sent a message to the Ufa Kremlin attention of Iosif Borisovich Petrov, Grantville Desk, Embassy Bureau, Ufa.

Dear Cuz
Have package. Need escort.
Gregory

It didn't take long till they got a message back.

Wait there.

An hour later, a captain showed up. "Gregory Petrov?"

Gregory looked up, and the captain came toward them. He was a tall man, six feet at least, with a short beard and a pressed uniform. It had ribbons on the right breast, five of them and, fresh from the academy, Gregory recognized them. Three were campaign ribbons, the river campaign that delayed the riverboats, the battle of Kazan, and the relief of Ufa. That last was a bit silly. They had marched out to relieve Ufa, but the Muscovy forces were already retreating. But the captain had a bronze star and a purple heart, and neither of those were jokes at all.

Gregory jumped up and saluted. It was a captain, after all, and Gregory had been in the Moscow Military Academy until three days ago.

The captain grinned a little, and returned the salute. "Welcome to Kazan, son. General Mazlov wants to have a chat before we put you on a boat to Ufa."

Gregory swallowed. Ivan Mazlov wasn't as famous as General Tim, but he was pretty famous. At least at the Military Academy.

Alla wondered if Mazlov, who was, after all, the son of a baker, would have a halo. The way Gregory was acting, he ought to.

* * *

Alla wasn't sure whether to be impressed or not impressed by General Ivan Mazlov. He was polite and amiable, as was Major Grachyov.

They both wanted to know everything they knew about the situation in Moscow. Both from Alla's perspective of living the last year in the servant's quarters, and from Gregory's about how things were going in the academy.

The general smiled when Gregory admitted that he'd gotten Mazloved in his first week in the Academy.

"What does that mean?" Alla asked.

It was Major Grachyov who answered. "It's a scam that the general here and General Boris Timofeyevich Lebedev came up with. The other players thought they were playing against Tim, but they were actually playing Ivan."

"But I thought it was General Tim who was the military genius?"

"Oh, he is," General Mazlov said. "Just ask any of the ladies of Kazan."

"Will someone explain what's going on, please?" Alla asked.

General Mazlov looked at her and said, "That's a little hard to explain. I've known Tim for years, and there are different kinds of intelligence. Different kinds of genius, if you will. I have the sort that loves to read and is really good at wargames or sitting comfortably in a war room and giving orders. But Tim, General Lebedev, has what William Tecumpseh Sherman called 'three AM brains.' Well, he said 'three AM courage,' but for our purposes, it's basically the same thing. You can wake Tim at three in the morning, tell him his army is under attack, and he'll ask the right questions, and give the right orders. If you're going into a real battle, you'd rather be facing me. If you're playing a war game, you'd rather face Tim."

Major Grachyov snorted. "In either case, you'd rather face Ismailov."

"Sucking up time is over, Major." Ivan said. "And don't underestimate Ismailov. He made a mistake outside Ufa, but it was the sort of mistake anyone might make. And I doubt he'll make that one again."

They talked through the meal and it was interesting. Then, as they were leaving, General Mazlov said, "Gregory, when you meet General Lebedev in Ufa, tell him 'I don't think it's soup yet.' "

"Yes, sir," Gregory said, "though I don't know what that means."

"That's all right. Tim will."

Location: Ufa
Date: July 26, 1637

Ufa was under construction. That was the only way to describe it. Everywhere you looked, people were building stuff. Buildings, sewers, roads, fences, defensive works. The steam boat they'd arrived on was immediately boarded by stevedores pushing wheelbarrows up onto the steam boat empty and taking them back down with Dacha cement or sand or gravel. Ufa was a city of wood that intended to be a city of concrete by winter.

That frenetic activity was mirrored in the court noble who met them on the docks five minutes after they docked. "Sorry I'm late," said the teenager. "I had to stop by Osip's to order sandwiches for the work crew on the west wall."

As they were escorted around and through the crush of people all going about what were apparently very important jobs, the court noble, whose name they didn't catch, explained that Osip was the owner of the best, well, the fourth best restaurant in Ufa. That he made a great black bread, ham, and cabbage hoagie, and with the labor shortage being what it was, even the czar's court had to cater to the workers a little bit.

✳ ✳ ✳

Once Alla and Gregory were in the Kremlin itself, things calmed down to simply frantic. They reached the czar's offices and were told to go wait somewhere else. Czar Mikhail was booked solid for the next three hours.

Gregory said, "Perhaps we could go see Cousin Iosif. Iosif Petrov, in the Embassy Bureau. He runs the Grantville desk. I have some letters for him."

"Excellent idea," the secretary said.

Apparently no one had time for introductions. If you mattered, you were expected to already know who they were.

149

* * *

Iosif was yelling at someone named Ivan when they were brought in. He looked over at them. "Hi, Gregory. You've grown. You and Miss Lyapunov wait in my office. I won't be a minute."

* * *

Five minutes later, Iosif came in. "Sorry. That took longer than I thought it would." He shrugged. "Everything does. But it's vital to get it right."

"What took too long, if you can tell me?" Gregory asked.

"Nothing secret. A message decrypt for the Dacha from Papa. Speaking of which, I understand you have some papers for me?"

"Yes, though I'm not so sure about why a Russian translation of *Basic Electrical Component Design* would be so vital to your office."

"Good. If you couldn't figure it out, probably—well, possibly— no one else will. Did anyone ask you about it?"

"No one so much as examined our bags."

"Good. If they don't know we have it, it's good."

"But Cousin, you can buy this book at the Gorchakov Dacha Bookstore for three rubles." Three rubles was a lot for a book, well over a hundred USE dollars. But it wasn't like you locked such a book up in a safe.

"It's a code book!" Alla blurted.

Everything stopped. Well, the muted roar of activity from outside Iosif's office continued unabated. But in the office, it seemed

150

everything stopped, while Gregory looked at her in confusion and Iosif in surmise.

"I think you and your new mother are going to get along famously," Iosif said after a few moments of consideration.

Alla felt herself stiffen. *What? Did this man think she would—* Her thoughts froze in their tracks as she remembered that this man's father was Boris Petrov and Boris Petrov had warned her not to make assumptions about Miroslava Holmes. After backtracking a little, her thoughts started up again. *He isn't talking about the whore. He's talking about the detective. Maybe?*

"You need to work on your poker face, Alla, but it's good to know that Vasilii isn't the only bright member of your family. Yes, it is indeed a code book and a code book for the transmission of technical data that the Sheremetev government in Moscow would rather we not have. Quite a lot of that book is numbers and equations which will allow us to tell the boffins over in the Dacha precisely what is and isn't working back in Moscow. And, for that matter, what is and isn't working in Grantville, Magdeburg, even Amsterdam, Venice, and Paris. About three-quarters of the most vital intelligence in this day and age is technical. And I have a stack of messages from sources all over Russia that I will decrypt using this book. Things that we don't want Sheremetev to know that we know.

"Where is he, by the way?"

"No one's heard from him since shortly after Salqam-Jingar Khan joined the USSR," Gregory said.

"There are rumors that he's in Poland, even rumors that he's in negotiations with King Wladislaw," Alla said.

"Where did you hear that?" Gregory asked.

"In the kitchen of your father's house," Alla told him, to Gregory's chagrin and Iosif's amusement.

"It's true, Gregory," Iosif said. "You often get the best intelligence from the servants. Of course, you also often get crap from them as well. The trick is separating one from the other." He looked them over, then continued. "I'm glad you got here safely. But here, or rather in the czar's office, is where your journey together is going to end.

"Miss Alla Lyapunov is going to be going on to stay with her new parents in the State of Kazakh with an escort of streltzi appropriate to her family's station. By the way, your new parents have both been enobled by the khan, so you're going to have to deal with that. And someone else got killed in the khan's moving city, so your new mother is going to be busy dealing with that.

"Meanwhile, Gregory, you've had a year in the academy at the Kremlin, is that right?"

"Fourteen months."

"Okay. General Lebedev is probably going to grab you for his staff, so you're going to be staying right here. But all of that's going to happen after Alla here is officially and publicly presented to Czar Mikhail and Czarina Evdokia tonight."

Alla found herself wondering what a— what Miroslava Holmes did in investigating a murder.

CHAPTER 11: THE POP AND DROP

Location: Khan's Moving City, South of Druzhba
Date: July 17, 1637

The body was identified as Erasyl Iskakov Bey, and he'd put up a fight. Miroslava pointed at scuffs in the dirt and at a boot print . . . well, the heel of a boot print that was clearly defined in the droppings of a goat. She had Vasilii take a close up of that. The heel was made of wood or bone, and it had been done by a competent boot maker, but the positioning of the nails wasn't completely even. The boot could be matched if they could find it. From just the boot print, it was impossible to know the wealth of the wearer. He wore riding boots, but everyone in Kazakh wore riding boots. Men, women, children, the rich, the poor, and more than a few slaves.

There was a bruise on his neck, but it was hard to tell if it was the result of the grip of a hand or a blow. "I don't believe you could tell all the things Conan Doyle said you could, just from looking, Cousin Sherlock," Miroslava muttered. "Nor any of the other detectives in books. There is too much variation caused by other factors." She was thinking of things like whether a major blood vessel had burst, how long after the choking or blow the person died and the blood stopped flowing. All sorts of things that made pure forensics less science and more guessing game. She wished she could do DNA, then wondered if DNA was as much a guessing game as the rest. But even while she was wondering about that, she was carefully tiptoeing around the crime scene, trying to see all the clues that she could without disturbing anything.

Finally, she stood up. There was a crowd being held back by streltzi and Kazakh guards, but looking on curiously.

"We have the pictures. You can take the body now," she told the Kazakh commander.

"Who killed him?" the commander asked. He'd been there when she'd exposed Nazar, and was apparently expecting her to solve the case right now. She looked at the ground at his feet. partly because she was still very uncomfortable looking at people's faces, and partly because until this case was solved, she would be looking at everyone's foot print.

"I don't know yet. We have a good set of fingerprints, but I don't know who to compare them to yet."

"Compare them to everyones!"

"Shall we start with yours?" Vasilii asked.

"What? No, of course not! You can't suspect me? I'm not a thief."

"We don't know if this was about theft yet," Miroslava said. "It might be political. It might be personal. It might be some combination of all three." Miroslava was looking at other people's feet as they moved around. The commander's boot prints hadn't matched the one in the goat dung. But she didn't say that. Vasilii was doing something social. She could tell that much, though she had no idea what.

* * *

Vasilii, an avid reader of procedural crime stories and a delegate to the constitutional convention, was familiar with the up-time American Bill of Rights and more importantly the Section of Civil Rights in the USSR constitution. He also knew that most of the states in the up-time America had had their own bills of rights. He wanted the State of Kazakh to have a bill of rights. And he wanted those rights to be universally applied. He'd heard Brandy Bates Gorchakov expound on Plessy versus Ferguson too many times to want to see some idiot judge proclaiming a peasant has no rights that a noble is bound to respect. And here was a test case. *The* test case. The one that would be looked at forever as the model for the Kazakh state's Section of Rights. Now all they needed was for Miroslava to solve the case without violating anyone's rights to prove it could be done.

Once the body was taken away, he and Miroslava went back to the *khibitkha*.

"What was that about? Why did you ask that man if we should start with his fingerprints? His boots didn't match the boot heel in the goat droppings."

"That's probable cause. And whether the police in Kazakh have to have probable cause to take incriminating evidence has yet to be determined. But this case will determine it. You solve it without violating anyone's civil rights, and we will be halfway to a Section of Civil Rights in the Kazakh constitution."

"*If* I solve it. If it was a random murder for profit, a mugging, I may not be able to. Muggings are the hardest cases to solve. There isn't necessarily any connection between the killer and the victim. That means that there is no trail between them." Then she shrugged. "I don't know why you care. The Section of Rights protects the guilty more than the innocent."

"I know, and that's the secret. It was before we met, at a party during the constitutional convention. The Section of Rights was being debated and I'd read a bunch of mysteries where the rights of the accused were making things harder for the investigators. So I asked Brandy Gorchakov about why they were a good idea if they protected the guilty. She'd had a bit too much wine, and she leaned over and whispered wine in my face. 'That's the secret,' she said. 'They're there to protect the guilty.' I didn't know what she was talking about, but I couldn't forget what she said.

"A few days later, I asked her again. And she explained it. The Bill of Rights was written by criminals, for criminals. And our Section of Civil Rights was written by criminals. According to Sheremetev,

Mikhail is under a spell. Bernie, Brandy, Vladimir, and all the delegates to the convention were criminals, including me.

"From the moment I got onto that steam boat at the Gorchakov Dacha, I was a traitor to Holy Mother Russia as Sheremetev saw things. I still am. I have been accused of treason twice now, and duly convicted in absentia both times by a Russian court back in Moscow. The first time was for running off to Ufa. And they only bothered with me because of my family. The second time was for attending the constitutional convention.

"And those courts could do that because I didn't have the right to face my accusers and argue my case. Because they could just take evidence against me and leave out anything that supported my case. Like the fact that the czar of Russia asked me to come, and how can it be treason if the czar asked? Oh, and by the way, you are probably going to be convicted of treason by the Sheremetev government, if you haven't been already, once you marry me."

"*If* I marry you. We still have to find out what the czar wants us to do in regard to your inheritance."

At that point, they sent off their message to the czar. Then Vasilii was called to a meeting with the khan and, accompanied by Sergeant Leonid Vetrov, who was part of their contingent of streltzi, Miroslava started interviewing everyone who knew Erasyl Iskakov Bey. They also sent off the crime scene film to Ufa to be processed.

Location: Khan's Moving City, South of Druzhba
Date: July 17, 1637

Kausar, Erasyl Iskakov Bey's wife, wasn't exactly heartbroken. She spoke Cantonese quite well, as well as Kazakh and Arabic, but she didn't speak Russian and Miroslava's Kazakh was still new. Miroslava's eidetic memory applied to sounds as well as sight, but the ability to remember a sound isn't the ability to reproduce it, nor is it the ability to tell "a" from "ay" from "au." And, especially, it's not something that Miroslava could do on the fly. For that matter, she was going to have to go through her memory of Kausar's words and compare them to the words she knew before she understood what Kausar was saying. In the meantime, there was a Kazakh cavalryman assigned as her translator.

The conversation, if you could call it that, went like this.

"Hello, Kausar. This is Miroslava—"

"I know who she is. Take her away. I don't talk to infidels."

Miroslava knew "infidel." She'd been hearing it often since she and Vasilii arrived. She knew "talk" and "don't," so she had a decent idea of the jist of Kausar's comments.

"The khan has—"

"The khan is a spoiled boy . . ." Then, apparently realizing that she'd crossed a line, "Oh, all right."

They went into the yurt, which was large and well appointed with embroidered wall hangings and a comfortable couch. There was a fire in the fireplace in the center and a pot of something that smelled spicy and good over the fire. There were lamps. They were neither the Coleman's or the older aladdin style lamps, but instead were wicked lamps with glass chimneys. They provided fill light in the nooks, but most of the light in the yurt came through the hole in the center of the roof.

Kausar went to a chair in front of an embroidery stand and, pointedly, didn't wave them to the couch or ask them to sit. Instead she said, "Ask your questions."

Which Miroslava had a pretty good guess at.

Sanzhar, the cavalryman who had been assigned to Miroslava by the khan, translated, adding "please," another word that Miroslava knew in Kazakh, but which hadn't been in what Kausar had said.

Miroslava asked. Sanzhar translated, Kausar answered or evaded. Sanzhar translated again and tried to make Kausar's responses less offensive, in the process obscuring some of what she said. It made for a very frustrating interview process and quite a bit of what Miroslava learned about Kausar's relationship with Erasyl she didn't find out until she was back in the *khibitkha* going over her mental notes.

Kausar cordially despised her husband. He was a gambler and a drunk, and not someone she would have married if she'd had a choice. But her family and his had wanted the marriage for political reasons. Her's was based in the capital, fairly strict in their adherence to Islam, and politically connected. His family was based in the plains and controlled a lot of land and a lot of cattle, but needed "respectability."

She was not a fan of Russians, who were profoundly uncivilized compared to the Chinese, who she did admire. She was a Muslim of

Shavgar, and was devout, avoiding alcohol and following the dietary rules scrupulously. Her husband hadn't been. She was almost certainly not the murderer herself. Her feet, which were in slippers in the yurt, were probably too small to match the boot print.

But that didn't mean that she hadn't arranged the murder. She certainly had motive. She didn't just disapprove of her husband's lifestyle. She disapproved of his politics, which favored the Russian statehood.

She thought he'd been murdered by one of his gambling buddies. They played a dice game, as well as betting on horse races and cock fights.

✳ ✳ ✳

After her interview with Kausar, Miroslava interviewed the bey's friends, and to a great extent, ended up in agreement with Kausar about their character. They were not all that different than the customers at the Happy Bottom, loud, grabby and hadn't bathed nearly recently enough. In that, they were worse than the customers at the Happy Bottom, saunas not being big in Kazakh culture, at least not away from the towns.

All in all, it was a frustrating week. A lot of footprints examined, and no suspects. She did learn rather a lot about Erasyl Iskakov Bey's life, politics, and friends. He wasn't exactly smart. More cunning. He was in favor of statehood, because while his clan did have a lot of cattle and therefore a lot of cavalry, it wasn't well positioned for taking over. His horses had excellent blood lines, his cattle were of good breeds. His family and clan . . . not so much. Having no real shot at replacing the khan, he figured the best thing for his clan was to promote a stable government and get rich on the opportunity provided by the Russian market.

On a personal basis, he liked gambling, drinking, and avoiding his "harridan of a wife." It wasn't a marriage made in heaven.

Location: Khan's Yurt, South of Druzhba
Date: July 17, 1637

Vasilii entered the Salqam-Jangir Khan's yurt and the first thing he heard was, "When will Miroslava solve the murder?"

"I don't know, Your Highness," Vasilii said, his eyes still adjusting to the relative dimness of the yurt. It wasn't actually dark, but outside the sky was bright blue and the sun was intense. As his eyes adjusted, he saw the khan, Sultan Togym, and Jaroslav Vinokurov, the new cartographer gathered around a map of the rail line, and therefore knew exactly what the discussion was about. Togym wanted the rail line in one place and Jaroslav said it would be easier to put it somewhere else.

"I don't even know that she will find the murderer. Some cases do go unsolved, you know. Even some of Miroslava's."

"So why aren't you fingerprinting everyone? I had Sanzhar Bey in here, insisting that we fingerprint all the criminals in the city."

"Very well, Great Khan. We will start with your fingerprints. They will then be on file to be compared with any fingerprints found at any crime scene from now until the end of time. Well, at least until you die. They might eliminate you as a suspect after you are dead and buried. But in the meantime, you should figure on being called in by the local prosecutor every time a kopek gets lost anywhere you've ever been."

"They wouldn't dare," Togym insisted.

"Oh, yes, they would," Salqam-Jangir Khan said. "And not even because they were out to get me, though many of them will be. Mostly they will be doing it so that they can prove that they are independent of my influence."

"Yes, Your Highness, and if they are out to get you, they will get you. I remember from a book I read once. Even a half competent prosecutor will be able to get a grand jury to convict a ham—" Vasilii stopped then. He was Russian Orthodox and ate ham sandwiches on a regular basis, but Salqam-Jangir Khan was Muslim, and Vasilii hadn't had any ham since he started on this mission. Perhaps in this company a ham sandwich might well be presumed to be guilty. He shrugged and continued. "—sandwich of murder, because the prosecutor gets to decide which evidence is relevant."

"What's a grand jury?" Togym asked.

"That's going to take some explaining," Vasilii admitted and it was, especially since the Russian system didn't have them. What it had instead was judges who prosecutors had to convince that they had a case worth taking to trial. Which, Vasilii was convinced, was a better system, whatever Bernie and Brandy said.

He spent the next three hours explaining up-time USA jurisprudence as it compared to USE jurisprudence and to Russian jurisprudence. And equal protection under the law. "That one is going to be hard to get around. Because it's part of the USSR constitution. It's—"

"I know where it is, Vasilii," Salqam-Jangir Khan said. "I was there when it was put into the Section of Civil Rights. I remember sitting through Vladimir's speech on the Christ clause. 'For Jesus said, whatsoever you do to the least of these, you have done to me.' Islam respects Jesus, and I approve of the clause as a matter of principle. But you're saying that if a prosecutor can't take my fingerprints, he can't take a slave's."

"That's exactly what I'm saying. And just like the slave's vote can't be coerced, neither can his agreement to have his fingerprints taken. You don't need his master's permission, you need his."

"What if the slave wants to give his fingerprint, and the master is opposed to it?" Togym asked. And at their looks, continued. "It could happen. If, say, the master thought the slave was guilty, or the master thought someone else was guilty and didn't want the slave eliminated from suspicion."

"I don't think there's ever been a case that covered that contingency, Sultan Togym," Vasilii said. "My preference would be that it's the slave's choice in either direction."

"Mine too," Salqam-Jangir Khan said.

"On a personal basis, I too agree," Togym said, though Vasilii wasn't at all sure that he meant it. Togym was the one who really wanted to buy Stefan Andreevich and put him to work making AK 4.7s. He was hardly a shining light of abolition. "But how explicit do we want to be about it in the Kazakh state Section of Civil Rights? Because, as Vasilii points out, a court might find differently. On the other hand, we will need to get the Section of Civil Rights past the sultans. Which is, I am sure, why Vasilii here is pointing out that under USSR law, the same law will apply to you or me that will apply to a slave or a beggar on the streets of Shavgar. So those laws should be quite protective of our, and the beggar's, rights." He gave Vasilii a knowing look.

"If you will excuse me," said Jaroslav. "This is all outside my field and, as Bernie would say, above my pay grade."

"I've been saying that for months," Vasilii muttered as Jaroslav made a hasty exit from the yurt.

And for the next several hours Vasilii, Togym, and the khan worked on the Section of Civil Rights for the Kazakh state constitution.

✳ ✳ ✳

Over the next several days, the sultans and beys of the Kazakh clans, as well as elected representatives from the various clans who were usually, but not always, in complete agreement with their clan chiefs debated the inherent conflict between catching, and punishing, the bad guys and protecting the rights of the people.

The fact that whatever coercions they allowed prosecutors would be applicable to them was a hard pill for most of those men to swallow. And they were all men. This was being put together on the fly. And the notion that a woman or a slave could run for office hadn't quite sunk in in Kazakh yet.

However, there were a number of herders and, well, vacaros or cowboys, among those elected to the constitutional convention. And while they usually went along with their sultans and beys, in this they were very much on the side of equality before the law. Not all of them, but enough—when combined with the khan and the coalition of liberal sultans or beys—to make sure that one, there would be equality before the law, and two, the sultan wouldn't also be the prosecutor.

Once that was decided, the "necessary authority" of the prosecutors suddenly became quite a bit less necessary. The new constitution of the Kazakh state would have severe limits on the seizure of evidence without the consent of the owner, and against forced or coerced testimony. No one would be compelled to give evidence against themselves.

Which threw the ball back into Miroslava Holmes' court.

Could she solve the murder without compelling everyone in the camp to provide a full set of fingerprints?

For ten days there were no noticeable results and the convention moved on to other matters, cattle theft, conflicts between sultans, the elections of clan representatives versus city representatives. The extent to which the laws of Islam, specificly the dietary restrictions and the prohibition against alcohol, would be written into the laws of the state.

Vasilii made several speeches, arguing that that sort of question should be left to the legislature, and the state constitution, aside from limiting the power of the state, should concentrate on figuring out how the legislature would be formed.

But it was an issue that wouldn't go away, because it would be affected by the way that the government was chosen. The cities to the south and east were more strict in their devotion to Islam. The cowboys, as Vasilii was more and more thinking of those who followed their herds, were Muslim only in the sense that they used Islam as a cloak. They threw it over practices and rituals that dated back centuries before Islam had arrived on the steepes and called those practices Islam. So the question of the Koran as law versus religious freedom was very much a city folk versus country folk issue.

One that was exacerbated by the fact that there were more cowboys than city slickers, but in the present government, the city slickers had more power.

Every night, Vasilii informed Miroslava that he wanted to be back in Ufa, working on the airplane.

CHAPTER 12: APPRENTICE DETECTIVE

Location: Ufa
Date: July 27, 1637

Alla looked at the airplane and wasn't impressed. She'd seen the massive dirigibles, the *Czarina Evdokia* and *Czar Alexi*, and this airplane was tiny in comparison, even if it would carry sixteen passengers and three crew. She was being shown the facility because her "new father" was one of the chief designers on the project.

Vadim Ivanovich wiped his hands on a filthy rag, then held one hand out for Alla to take. A year ago she would have cringed. And, in a way, she still did, but she'd had her hands in chicken guts and pulled out the internal organs of pigs and sheep over the last year. She knew by now that hands could be washed. She took his hand.

He said, "Welcome to the Skunk Works."

Alla sniffed. "It doesn't smell that bad." And it didn't. There was the smell of pine resin and burning fuel, coal or something like it.

"It's one of Vasilii's up-timer things that he got from the books. Secret projects are called skunk works. Well, the places where you do secret projects are called skunk works. I don't know why and I doubt if Vasilii does. It's just something he picked up."

"If it's secret, why am I here?"

"Because you're going to give your new papa a full report on our progress. And you're going to give Salqam-Jangir Khan the same report, since you're going to be going there anyway." He shrugged and grinned at her. "After all, if you fall off a horse while you're out among the Kazakh, we're not much worse off." He grinned, and Alla was almost sure that he was joking. Almost.

"Don't worry too much. It's not going to be secret that much longer. We're getting close."

She looked at the airplane, and it looked finished. At least from the outside. "It looks finished."

"Oh, that's just the body. We had that done four months after we got to Ufa, and it only took that long because everyone was busy with other stuff. The body is just wood and goldbeater's skin. We considered canvas and doping, but we had all the experience from building the dirigibles, and we had the crew from Bor. You know, more than half the technical team from Bor came over to Czar Mikhail's side just after General Tim took the place. Most of them went to Hidden Valley, but enough stayed in Ufa to let us make a hard shell out of goldbeater's skin and resins over a wood frame."

Alla understood about half of what he was talking about. "Still, two months?"

"Sure. Look, an airplane frame is no more complicated than a dirigible frame, and it's a lot smaller. You have control runs, but those are just wires and gears to let the pilot pulling on a stick move the control surfaces. We had to know how to do all that to control a dirigible. We got the shape and properties of the wings from the Netherlands. The same place we got the design for the air cushion landing gear." He pointed at a skirt around a platform that was apparently some sort of . . . Alla didn't know what the stuff the skirt was made of was.

The explanation went on and eventually she was shown inside. This part was a lot less finished. There was a steam boiler in the central portion of the aircraft, between the pilot and the passenger compartments and it was hot because there was a fire in the boiler.

"This will be insulated with spun glass fibers to save fuel and to keep the passengers and crew from broiling.

"Kliment, are we up to steam?"

"Yes."

"Okay, let's test the left outboard engine."

There were, in the pilot's compartment, five levers, four in a row and a fifth that was behind them. Kliment, she guessed, got up from where he was looking at gauges and went to the space between two seats and pushed the one on the far left.

Vadim pointed out the window on the left side and Alla saw the propeller start to spin.

"We're losing pressure," Kliment shouted. He didn't really need to shout. The propeller wasn't making that much noise, even in the hanger.

"Darn," Vadim muttered, looking at the gauges. "We thought we had that leak fixed." He looked at Alla. "It's hard to see a steam leak in an engine next to a propeller because the wind blows the steam away. The only way to tell is by the gauges."

After some more discussion between Vadim and Kliment, they left.

Alla went back to her packing. But she had a lot to think about. Vasilii was an important man out here. And that was confusing, because bookworm Vasilii had always been an embarrassment to the family. Not a proper son of the house. Not a warrior or an important person in one of the bureaus. Just a fiddler with devices.

But now those devices were of interest to Czar Mikhail and apparently to Salqam-Jangir Khan.

The next morning, she left in a three car train. And that was another revelation. Kliment, who she'd met the day before, had been heavily involved in building the steam locomotive and the rail cars with their lowerable rail wheel, a steel wheel with a concave rim that could be lowered onto a wooden rail and take most of the weight of the train or the rail cars. They had a starting rail line that went almost a mile south from Ufa, crossing over a river to do it. Of course, at the end of the mile, they had to stop and lift the rail wheels and shift the power train to the wagon wheels and proceed much more slowly. But for that first mile they were traveling at a top speed of twenty-five miles an hour.

Location: Khan's Yurt, South of Druzhba
Date: July 27, 1637

Vasilii was seated in what he was coming to think of as his chair and had a glass of small beer in his hands, and the day's wrangling over who would get the vote in the "people's chamber" of the legislature was over for the day.

Salqam-Jangir Khan sipped his tea with honey and said, "So tell me about your new daughter, Vasilii."

"I don't know much, Your Highness. I think I've spoken to her half a dozen times in my life, and none of those were much more than 'how are you' followed by 'I'm fine.' I don't think her parents wanted my books and odd ideas influencing her."

"That I can well understand," Sultan Togym said. "The influence you're having on the women here is deeply concerning to half the men in the Constitutional Convention. Which is why we're having so much trouble getting them to agree to let women vote, in spite of the obvious benefits."

"Yes. You're afraid they will make up their own minds who to vote for," Vasilii agreed. "You're right. Sooner or later, they will. But they are going to do that, whatever you do here. Equality before the law means women too."

"Enough politics, Togym," Salqam-Jangir Khan said before Togym could complain again about Vasilii's and, more importantly, Miroslava's influence. "What are your plans for her? I understand she's of marriageable age?"

"Not in Russia. Well, not in my family anyway." A thought occurred to Vasilii. "And please put out the word that I won't react well to a marriage kidnapping. The bride price will probably include the head of the groom." Kidnapping brides wasn't common in Russia, though it did happen. It was rather more common in the clans that followed their herds. Almost a rite of passage.

"That seems a most unreasonable attitude," Sultan Togym said. "I don't approve of the practice, but boys will be boys."

"Boys will be *corpses* if they attempt to kidnap Alla," Vasilii said, and put his hand over the place where his pistol resided in a shoulder holster.

"I will spread the word. I just hope that they don't take it as a challenge," Sultan Togym said.

"Do that, Togym," Salqam-Jangir Khan said. "And include the fact that I won't be happy with the clan that makes it necessary for me to judge the case after Vasilii kills one of their idiot sons." Then he looked at Vasilii. "I also won't be happy with you."

"I hope it won't become necessary. But after learning what I know about Miroslava's experiences, and learning that several of the women in my own class don't feel that their situation was really all that different—"

"What?" Salqam-Jangir Khan asked.

"Whether your family sells you to be the brood mare for another family or a prostitute, you're still being sold. At least, that's what women such as Natasha Gorchakov and Zia Ivaneva Chernoff have told me.

"So Alla will have a say in who she marries and when. Though it won't be this year or next."

Location: Steam Train
Date: July 31, 1637

Alla was jerked to the side as the heavy wheels of the rail car encountered a rock and the whole rail car bumped over it. The "club" car—well, all the cars on the train—were designed to have most of their weight on a rail and the rest on a graded surface. They weren't well designed for traveling over hills and dales. Every minute or so the train, which was traveling at about three miles an hour, hit another rock or tree root or gopher hole, or who knew what, and jerked Alla half out of her seat. It would be all the way out of her seat, but she was belted in.

There was a table in the rail car and it too was designed so that its contents could be tied down. And the cargo in the two freight cars was tied down even harder. It wasn't like the builders of the engine and cars weren't aware of the problems. They talked to her about them in the evenings. Every evening they stopped at a radio telegraph station, usually about fifteen miles farther along their route, but sometimes if the ground was good, they would skip one and travel thirty miles in a day.

Still, at best, they weren't going as fast as a dispatch rider. But Alla had the case pictures for Miroslava and the designs for the new Bogatyr class of aircraft. Well, at least it was the Bogatyr class for now. Princess Irina was lobbying heavily for them to be named Polianitsa, the female version of the Bogatyr, just as strong and brave, but cleverer, Irina insisted, and Alla agreed.

But agreeing or not, the technical details of the steam-powered airplanes were a bit too much for Alla. She found them frustrating.

So, to avoid studying them, she was now studying the photographs of the murder that the strange woman called Miroslava was even now investigating in the camp, or moving city, of the Kazakh khan.

The pictures were fascinating in a gruesome sort of way. There were pictures of the knife wound in the man's side. Well, back. From the notes, the first blow was in the back on the man's left side, indicating that the attacker was probably left-handed. Probably, but not certainly. A right-handed man can hold a knife in his left hand. Maksim Borisovich Vinnikov, the pushy boy who had briefed her on the case before she left had pointed that out. Between gushing over how brilliant and beautiful and strange Miroslava Holmes was, and explaining how he was going to be a detective sergeant someday.

Maksim had pointed out that the reason for the close up photograph of the bootheel print in the animal dung with the ruler next to was that the boot print was probably of the boot of the killer "and see that nail on the left side. It's not just out of place. The head is bent over to the side a little."

Looking at the picture now, Alla wasn't convinced. It wasn't, after all, a picture of the bootheel. It was a picture of goat dung with an imprint of a bootheel in it. That extra little groove didn't need to be a bent nail. It could be a bit of grass that was attached to the bootheel when the fellow stepped in the dung. It could have been a piece of grass or a leaf that was sitting on the dung when the man stepped in it. Or just maybe it was a bent over nail head.

Along with the picture were measurements based on the ruler that—according to Maxim—Vasilii had put by the dung pile before he took the picture. Because the one thing in all the world that Miroslava Holmes wasn't good at was taking pictures.

The train car jerked again, and Alla almost lost her hold on the photograph. She cursed under her breath.

Then she went on to the next picture. This was of the fingerprint on the victim's armor with the bloody fingerprints displayed. Again there was the little ruler and the notes of the distance between the hooks and whorls of the fingerprints.

Location: Moving City of the Kazakh State
Date: August 3, 1637

Alla climbed down the two tall steps of the train car to see a city of yurts in the process of being built. Apparently they had moved yesterday after a stay of three days. They were now ten miles closer to the Aral Sea than they had been. The scouts and map makers were forging ahead and the city was lagging behind because the delays caused by the debates over the new state constitution were ongoing. There were men in turbans and armor with horses and bows, swords and jewels. There were women in pants and vests and tiaras. And even the yurts were embroidered. It was a colorful place, and the train was the center of attention.

And there was Cousin Vasilii, looking very much the same as he had the last time she'd seen him. It had been two, or maybe three, years ago at a family dinner. He'd already been working at the Gorchakov Dacha for a couple of years, and showed up in a shirt with zippers on display, with that silly clipboard in his pocket.

Now he was family, all the family she had left. And yet he wasn't. He wasn't her father or her mother, her brothers and sisters. She didn't know what to do or how to act.

There was a woman next to him. She was dressed very much as the women she'd seen at the Ufa Dacha dressed. But not quite. She was wearing pants that were tight enough so that it was clear they were pants, not the sort of split dresses that were the fashion. She was wearing makeup, but it was in the style that the czarina favored. She had auburn hair in a ponytail. And she was pretty. Really pretty. She made Alla feel drab and colorless just by being there.

Alla knew she had to be the famous Miroslava Holmes that everyone raved about. But she didn't look like a whore or a dancer. She wasn't half dressed in clothing that invited sex. She was . . . Alla didn't know what she was, and that confused and upset her.

Vasilii didn't wait for her to make up her mind. He walked up, took her hands, and said, "Welcome, daughter," and kissed her on both cheeks.

Alla didn't know what to say, but she knew that this virtual stranger wasn't her papa. But her lifetime of training kicked in, and she didn't blurt it out. Not knowing the politics of the situation and not knowing what to say, she said nothing.

Then Cousin Vasilii said in her ear, "Don't worry, Alla. We'll get through this, and then we'll have a long talk."

For the next hour or so, Alla was introduced to about a third of the state nobles of Kazakh as Alla Lyapunov, Vasilii's cousin and newly adopted daughter. Alla was a noble again, after a year as a kitchen drudge. And the strangest thing was that she wished she was back in the kitchen, being yelled at by Cook for searing the mushrooms.

* * *

Finally, back in the yurt, Miroslava listened as Vasilii drew out the girl. She was still far from comfortable in this sort of situation. She knew how to be a dancer and she knew how to be a detective. She didn't know, even a little bit, how to be a mother.

As Alla described life in the Petrov kitchen, it didn't seem too bad. Not as bad as a number of things she'd experienced. Then Vasilii got Alla to talk about the day her parents were killed. That was pretty bad.

Alla had spent most of her life learning how to be the wife of an upper level member of the service nobility. Then, the last year, learning how to be a kitchen maid. She hadn't had any training in how to be her own self.

That, at least, was something Miroslava could understand.

Vasilii said, "I know this isn't how you wanted your life to go, Alla, and I know Crazy Cousin Vasilii isn't the person that you would want in charge of your life and prospects. But, thanks to Sheremetev and his adherents, I'm . . . well, Miroslava and I are what you've got.

"We'll do the best we can for you. Now, tell me. Politics and family situation allowing, what do *you* want to do with your life?"

Miroslava could see by the girl's face that she had no notion of what to say to that. "You don't have to answer that question now. You have time, but it is a question to think about."

"I don't know. I know how to read and I know somewhat of how to cook using a Franklin stove, but I don't know how to do anything useful. Not like designing steam engines for airplanes."

Vasilii laughed. "When did that become useful, not the deranged pursuits of Crazy Cousin Vasilii?"

Miroslava could hear the bitterness in that question. Bitterness that Alla could only hear as accusation.

"It's not Alla's fault that your cousins didn't approve of you, Vasilii," Miroslava said more sharply than she'd intended. Then spoke to the girl. "Alla, Vasilii isn't mad at you. He's mad at the world because . . . well, I don't know why he's mad at the world, seeing as he's been rich and privileged his whole life long."

Vasilii looked at her for a moment, then grinned. "That's true enough. Compared to some, I have had a charmed life, especially since the Ring of Fire brought the up-timers and their knowledge. And she's right. I'm not mad at you. But I can tell you what I'm mad at. I'm mad at a world that doesn't value knowledge and hard work as much as it values the ability to beat on someone and take their stuff. Like this murderer that Miroslava is looking for. Or like Sheremetev. I don't like the fact that the world seems to reward the people who just take, rather than the people who make.

"And while the knowledge of the up-timers helps, especially the knowledge that knowing how to do stuff is valuable, not silly, the world is still like that. Three-quarters of the nobles in Kazakh are still convinced that because they can shoot a bow and swing a sword they are entitled to take anything they want from people who can't do that."

* * *

Alla sat there and listened to Crazy Cousin Vasilii and realized that, stripped of all the high-sounding rhetoric about noble heritage and good blood, about service to Holy Mother Russia and the natural rewards of that service, the attitude he was describing was precisely her father's attitude and, even more, her mother's. And she found herself wondering, just for a moment, if maybe Vasilii *should* be mad at her. Then, of course, she got mad at him. "Well, since you're the one who has that sword here, what are you going to do with me?"

Vasilii blinked. "I don't know. I've been trying to figure that out since Czar Mikhail told me that I had a living cousin, and if I was going to marry Miroslava, I should adopt her."

"Why . . . oh, *mestnichestvo.*" Alla looked a sneer at Miroslava. "You need an *acceptable* heir."

"I need an heir, period." Vasilii said with a hardness in his voice that wasn't there before. "Miroslava doesn't want to have children. But, yes, the book of *mestnichestvo* and the people who keep it will be happier with you as the next Lyapunov after me. And that will help the czar with the conservatives back in Moscow." Vasilii shrugged. "Help him a little. Most of those fossils won't change their minds, no matter what."

"Then why do you care? Why does Czar Mikhail?"

"Hope springs eternal. He'd rather persuade them than kill them." Vasilii took a breath. "Never mind that. I know that this wasn't your choice, but Miroslava and I will do our best for you." He stepped over to her, took her shoulders in his hands and looked her in the eye. "What do *you* want to do with your life?"

Alla didn't have a clue. She had no earthly idea what she wanted to do with her life. Up to now, she'd never had any choice. Not in the Petrov kitchen and not in the Lyapunov home where she'd grown up and Crazy Cousin Vasilii was held up as an example of what happens if you let children choose their own interest. "I don't know. I couldn't make heads or tails of the designs for the *Nastas'ya Nikulichna*."

"*Nastas'ya Nikulichna?*"

"Well, it's not named yet, and Irina wants the class of the plane to be the Polianitsa class. So the first one ought to be the greatest Polianitsa."

"Ah, clearly you're going to be a politician," Vasilii said with a grin.

And, almost in spite of herself, Alla grinned back.

"I did mostly follow the reports and the pictures from the murder case. And I don't think it's a bent over nail."

"You don't think what is a bent over nail?" Vasilii asked.

At the same time Miroslava asked, "What do you think it is?"

The pouch that held the pictures was on a table. And Alla guessed that the servants had put it there while they were meeting all the Kazakh nobles in camp. Alla went to it, and both Vasilii and Miroslava followed. She opened the pouch and pulled out the blow up of the impression in the goat droppings.

The bootheel had had seven nails holding it together. One right at the back, two more on either side and two across the front edge. The one on the left side closest to the back wasn't quite where it was supposed to be. It was a little in from the outer edge and rather than a circular hole it was a line in the goat dropping. Not a long line, but as though the nail had bent to the side on the last hammer stroke.

"What do you think it is?" Miroslava asked again.

"I think it's a bit of leaf or grass. Goats will eat anything and it doesn't always get fully, ah, processed, before it comes out."

Miroslava nodded. "Possibly. Which means we may be looking for a slightly misplaced nail, not a bent one."

"So maybe you're an apprentice detective," Vasilii said.

"Maybe," Alla said doubtfully.

Gorg Huff & Paula Goodlette

CHAPTER 13: POLITICS AND BOOT PRINTS

Location: Moving City of the Kazakh State
Date: August 4, 1637

The next morning, Alla accompanied Vasilii to consult with Salqam-Jangir Khan about the airplane and the steam train. Partly that was to give the khan a non-technical view of the two projects. But it was also to introduce her to the state politics of the Kazakh state.

Czar Mikhail had realized something that Vasilii and Miroslava hadn't. The resolution of Colonel Ivan Smirnov's murder had left both Vasilii and Miroslava as at least quasi-official Kazakh nobles. And as their adopted daughter, that rank would land on Alla, making her a connection between the USSR and the State of Kazakh.

He wanted her to get to know Salqam-Jangir Khan and his nobles. All this had been explained to Alla, not by the czar, but by the czarina.

So she was on her best charming-daughter-of-the-Russian-nobility behavior while she explained her tour of the "*Nastas'ya Nikulichna*," and its leak in the outboard engine.

"So Vasilii's toy still doesn't work?" Salqam-Jangir Khan grinned, and several of the nobles in the room laughed outright.

"No, Your Highness." Alla used the Russian title. "But it will soon. Vadim Ivanovich assures me of that, and I believe him. What I do know is that it will be ready long before the rail line reaches here, much less the Aral Sea."

"Yet you are here," Sultan Togym said, "brought by a steam train without rails."

Alla curtsied to the old man. "Yes, Sultan, but I would have traveled faster in a carriage with a change of horses every twenty miles or so. Much faster. But I went the first miles on a wooden rail line, and while I was on that, I traveled faster than a galloping horse. When the rail line gets here, when it gets to the Aral Sea, you will be able to move goods from Ufa to the Aral Sea in a day or two, not weeks. But even before that, when the '*Nastas'ya Nikulichna*' and her sisters are built and flying, you will be able to get from Ufa to the Aral Sea in hours." Alla wasn't sure of that, but she wasn't going to lose an argument just because she didn't know for sure that she was right.

"More importantly," Cousin Vasilii said, "the rail line won't let you scout the Zunghar Khanate or the movement of their troops, but with a—" He stopped and grinned at Alla. "—*polianitsa* equipped with a radio, you will know where they are in real time."

Alla knew that in the time that Vasilii and Miroslava had been in Kazakh, the Zunghar Khanate had launched several raids on Kazakh territory, apparently testing the waters. They needed the ability the airplanes would provide. They needed it yesterday.

At least they had heard about the raids in the time that Vasilii and Miroslava had been in Kazakh. Even by post rider, it took time for word to reach across the state of Kazakh.

"What we need are the radios," Sultan Togym said. "By the time we hear of a raid, the Zunghars are back in their own lands. Meanwhile, we are here, talking about whether my blacksmith's daughter should be able to run for congress."

"She should," Alla said promptly. After all, she wasn't going to let the lack of facts keep her from expressing her opinion.

"She's five years old," Togym said.

"I didn't say you had to vote for her, Sultan," Alla insisted, to general laughter.

And the discussions continued. Alla found them interesting.

✳ ✳ ✳

The end of the day's session arrived and plans were made for the wedding of Miroslava Holmes to Vasilii Lyapunov. Alla still wasn't at all sure how she felt about that. Miroslava wasn't the white faced strumpet that she had expected, but she was weird, and Alla by now was feeling like she was the guardian of the family reputation. It wasn't like Vasilii was going to do it.

But no one was going to listen to her.

* * *

In truth, Miroslava might have listened. She wasn't feeling all that comfortable with the whole situation. She didn't know how to act like a noblewoman. Not even of the service nobility, much less the higher nobility, which if the Lyapunov family wasn't quite, they almost were. She also didn't know how to be married. It wasn't like she could host a dinner party.

At this point, the upcoming wedding was distracting her from the case.

So things went for three days.

Location: Moving City of the Kazakh State
Date: August 7, 1637

Vasilii and Alla were coming out of the day's conference. Not the constitutional convention, the conference that followed the day's convention, where the khan's government dealt with the restiveness to the south and the increasing raids by the Zunghars to the east.

Suddenly, Alla stopped and Vasilii took three more steps before he noticed. Then he stopped, looked around, and saw her staring at the ground. He followed her gaze, and in a bare patch of earth there was a boot print. Actually, there were three boot prints. But one of them had the displaced nail that Miroslava and he had been looking for. He followed the direction of the heel print, and this time in front of it was the print of the rest of the boot sole. That gave the size. Boots in the seventeenth century weren't made in factories to agreed on sizes. But boot makers, shoe makers in general, did have lasts, forms used to base a boot on. But lasts were made by the shoemaker in the size that that particular shoemaker thought that they ought to be. There was no universal size ten. Yuri might have one size ten and Pavel a different one. But with just the heel, they didn't know enough to identify the maker of that particular boot.

"Stop!" Vasilii shouted in Kazakh. The reason he shouted was because a food vendor was about to push her push cart over the boot print. But the results were not what he was expecting.

The food vendor stopped all right, and so did just about everyone in earshot. Including one fellow about twenty paces away, who stopped, looked back, saw Alla and Vasilii looking at the ground, and started running.

"Stop him!" Alla shouted, pointing.

The moving city of the convention was a big place, much bigger than a stationary city of the same population would be, because while the nobles tried to get their yurts or wagons as close to the khans as they could, the hangers on and the independents who came to provide clothing, boots, food, and drink to the khan's court and the convention attendees could put their yurts and wagons as far away from the center of camp as they wanted. And were encouraged by their "betters" to put them a bit farther away than that. There were also no two story yurts.

Still, it was a city. A lot of people in reasonably close proximity of each other, and in the case of the Kazakhs, a lot of cattle, sheep, horses and the occasional camel.

When Vasilii shouted, there were thirty or forty people in earshot. When Alla shouted, there were a dozen people who might have stopped him, but Alla was a young teenager and she shouted in Russian, not Kazakh. People looked, but didn't act. At least not in time.

He ran behind a yurt and disappeared.

But they had complete footprints now. Several of them, and a rough description of the man. He was five six or seven, with a round, fairly Asian face, and black hair and eyes. And he'd been seen running by dozens of people.

Miroslava was called and descriptions were taken, boot prints were measured. At which point, Alla's theory that the bent over nail was in fact a piece of grass was disproven or, at least, lost a lot of credibility. A piece of grass wouldn't still be there days later.

It took them into the evening to find the man's wagon. It wasn't a yurt. It was a wagon and was one of three that were traveling together. His name was Daniyar and he was a gambler by profession. He owned several fighting cocks and made his living through his skill with dice and his bird's skill in the ring.

All that was enough to take before the khan and get a warrant to examine his wagon. The wagon yielded several fingerprints, some of which matched the bloody prints on the armor.

They had their man.

Well, no.

They knew who their man was. He'd realized he was caught as soon as Vasilii shouted "Stop!"

He'd taken his horse and made a run for it. The other thing about the traveling town of the convention was that it had no walls and there really wasn't any way of keeping people from leaving if they wanted to.

Location: Moving City of the Kazakh State
Date: August 8, 1637

Witnesses were called. The hearing was being held in front of the khan's yurt and in the presence of a fairly large crowd. Daniyar was a moderately well known gambler and several people were aware that he'd been very upset by the death of his prize cock, Nurislam. Nurislam was killed in a fight against what should have been a weaker bird and Daniyar suspected the other bird had poison on his beak. Not considered sporting, but something that happened fairly often. It was known that Erasyl Iskakov Bey had bet heavily on the bird that killed Nurislam.

Then, after Erasyl Iskakov Bey had been killed, Daniyar stopped complaining. He also had more money.

"And you didn't feel the need to inform the authorities of these things?" Slaqam-Jangir Khan asked the woman who was testifying.

She looked terrified, but didn't answer.

Miroslava looked at the khan. "I suspect that if someone suggested that she inform the authorities of the murder of her son, she'd not do it.

"The authorities usually don't appreciate being bothered by . . . the sort of people I was back in Ufa. They, you, look at someone like her or me and bring out the torturer to get a confession and 'solve' the case."

"Which," Vasilii said, "is another reason you need a strong protection of individual rights in the state constitution. If you ever hope to have women like Sofia here come forward, they are going to need some assurance that they will be treated fairly."

"Are you suggesting I am unfair?" Salqam-Jangir Khan asked in an ominous voice.

"Of course you are unfair," Miroslava said in her distracted way. "Everyone is unfair."

"Which is why we need those protections," Vasilii said. "I remember during the convention in Ufa, we were reading about the up-timer Founding Fathers and someone repeated a quote from someone I don't know who said, 'Any government would serve if all men were angels, but if men were angels, no government would be needed.' But men aren't angels. Even khans aren't angels. That is why we need governments and why those governments must have restrictions placed upon them."

Meanwhile, Sofia was looking like a mouse at a cat convention. And Alla was starting to see Cousin Vasilii's point. She was also starting to wonder if maybe, just maybe, her parents might have been wrong about Crazy Cousin Vasilii.

* * *

As for Daniyar, he got clean away.

As for Alla, she was finding her short experience with solving crime to be most unsatisfying. Not only did the killer escape, she didn't know if her theory about the shoe nail was right or wrong. The boot in question had escaped on the killer's right foot. It was bad enough that the bad guy got away, but there were so many unanswered questions. Did his boot have a bent nail or not? Did he kill Erasyl Iskakov Bey over the dead rooster or to get the money and rings he had on him? Was it planned or spur of the moment?

For all they knew, he might have killed Erasyl Iskakov Bey over a woman or even in self defense if the fight had started over the rooster, and just took the money after Erasyl was dead.

Location: Moving City of the Kazakh State
Date: August 18, 1637

The rail line was mapped out most of the way to the Aral Sea, but the convention was still less than a third of the way there. But the convention was finished. Most of the sultans had signed the documents, but there were three holdouts, in spite of the clear majority in favor of it. All three of the holdouts had their territories to the south and east of Kazakh and that was worrying.

Then they got word over the radio.

**THE NASTAS'YA NIKULICHNA CRASHED.
GET BACK HERE.**

Gorg Huff & Paula Goodlette

CHAPTER 14: A WEDDING AND HOME

Location: Moving City of the Kazakh State
Date: August 18, 1637

Vasilii took the radio telegraph to the khan and started talking about arrangements to leave.

"Not yet," Salqam-Jangir Khan said. "First, you will be married here. With Us, before all my sultans and beys. Well, all those that are here."

"Salqam—"

"It won't take long," Salqam-Jangir Khan insisted. "And I want it done here first. You can have another after you get back to Ufa. But you're my nobles as well as Mikhail's, and this will be done properly by Kazakh custom."

Vasilii looked at the khan's grinning face, and knew it was a lost cause.

There were compromises that had to be made.

In a normal Kazakh wedding, the bride is presented to the groom's family in a ceremony called a *betashar*. She shows proper deference, then her veil is lifted and the mother-in-law kisses her cheek, welcoming her into the family, and puts a white scarf on her head to proclaim her a married woman.

But Vasilii only had his cousin, now his adopted daughter. So Alla was the one who kissed Miroslava's cheek, welcoming her into the family. This was followed by several hours of feasting, in this case with a fair chunk of the upper nobility of the state of Kazakh.

The next part of the ceremony, the *Neke Qiyu*, required even more adjustment. And that was the part that Salqam-Jangir Khan was after. Because *Neke Qiyu* was the part where the mullah read from the Koran and asked both bride and groom to profess their faith in Islam.

Or at least that was how it had been done when there wasn't freedom of religion in the State of Kazakh. Kazakh still had a state religion, Sunni Islam, but it also had freedom of religion and the freedom of religion was turning out to be more of an issue than anyone had really expected. Some of the more "rural" clans were, it turned out, less devoted to Islam than anyone had thought, once they actually had a choice.

So Salqam-Jangir Khan had made a compromise with the mullahs of Kazakh. They got to read from the Koran, but the bride and groom weren't required to profess faith in Islam.

The compromise didn't actually satisfy anyone, but compromises often fail to satisfy.

Location: En Route to Ufa
Date: August 20, 1637

The train bumped and Alla was jerked around. Fortunately, the train had two freight cars as well as the passenger car that Alla had ridden in on the way from Ufa. One of those freight cars had been converted into a bridal suite for Vasilii and Miroslava.

Which Alla found to be a relief. She knew what they were doing back there and didn't want to be there while they did it. But, in spite of herself, every time the train hit a bump, she imagined them flung about in various stages of undress.

Alla wondered what her life was going to be like. There was no going back to the life she'd had in Moscow. But she was again the daughter of a deti boyar house in the Russian Empire. And suddenly her family—Vasilii, Miroslava and her—were now actually of higher rank than her parents had been.

What, Alla wondered, *is life as a Russian noble, in this new world, going to be like?*

NOTES

Mestnichestvo: family ranking system

Deti boyars—the retainers of the great houses, the phrase "Deti boyars" means boyar's sons.

Dvoriane—the service nobility. People who work in the bureaus or the army. Nobles like Vasilii are often both. In Vasilii's case, his family is actually related to the Cherakasky family and has had middle to upper level positions in the army and the bureaus for generations.

Zunghar Khanate: relatively new as a khanate, the Zunghar tribes are also heirs of Mongol Empire and occupy the lands between China and the Kazakh.

Turkistan/Shavgar is the capital of the Kazakh Khanate. Which name it was called by is vague in the histories, but we called it Shavgar in 1637: The Volga Rules. At the same time in history, the Kazakh khanate was mostly herders who moved with their herds and wagon trains that amounted to moving towns.

Auyl: A nomadic village following the herd

Khibitkha: A large wheeled platform on which a yurt is built. A mobile home for a world without roads. They could require as many as thirty oxen to pull them.

Character List

Baranov, Pavel: Detective, Ufa

Blinov, Ilya: streltzi lieutenant

Bobrov, Oleg: Teenager at Ufa Dacha, tutoring Miroslava

Brezhnev, Lukyan: Protocol Officer, Ufa Kremlin

Budanov, Simeon: head of Ufa Embassy Bureau

Buturlin, Timofei Fedorovich: Colonel, Garrison Commander, Ufa

Dobryn, Stefania: surveyor assistant to Vinokurov

Drozdov, Elena: Owner of The Happy Bottom. Insists on being called Madam.

Drysi: Telegraph operator

Egor Petrovich: Employee of the gun shop

Esim: Tatar doctor

Fyodorov, Viktor Bogdonovich: Radio manager at Dacha station

Gorchakov, Brandy: Up-timer, counselor to the royal family

Gorchakov, Vladimir Petrovich: Boyar, Counselor to Czar Mikhail

Holmes, Miroslava: Our Sherlock Holmes, starts out as a bar girl. She has hazel eyes and auburn hair, she is five seven.

Karimov, Aidar: cousin of Bey Nazar and tribal chief

Kotermak, Yuriy: Ufa city Garrison Sergeant.:

Lyapunov, Alla: 14 year old, last of the line, hiding in Moscow

Lyapunov, Vasilii: Engineer geek, Ufa Dacha: He is five foot nine and weighs around a hundred and seventy pounds, he normally wears combat boots in a design copied from up-time US military jump boots. They have laces and a hardened toe, and are usually polished to a high gloss. Russian-made jeans, usually in black or dark green, and a lighter colored tunic or undercoat for indoors. He has a high forehead or a slightly receding hairline. His hair is dark brown and he has freckles. His close trimmed beard is also brown but lighter than his hair. He has a bump on his nose and slightly crooked teeth but not badly crooked.

Matvey: A beat cop

Mazlov, Ivan: brevet general, czar's army

Nazar, Bey: works for Salqam-Jangir Khan

Petrov, Gorgy: relative of Boris Ivanovich Petrov

Petrov, Iosif Borisovich: son of Boris Ivanovich Petrov, Grantville Desk of Ufa Kremlin.

Petrov, Nadia: daughter of Gorgy

Olga Petrovichna: effectively the mayor of Ufa

Rayana: Kazakh slave

Ruzukov, Stefan Andreevich: Factory owner in Ufa and recently advanced to dvoriane

Ruzukov, Vera Sergeevna: Delegate to Constitutional Convention, called "The Honorable."

Salqam-Jangir Khan: head of the Kazakh Khanate

Simmons, Tami: Nurse and Surgeon General for Mikhail's Russia

Smirnov, Ivan: Colonel and surveyor

Togym: Sultan, General, Kazakh leader

Vasin, Damir: Kazan streltzi

Vedenin, Dimitri: Kazan streltzi sergeant

Vinnikov, Maksim Borisovich: Teenaged reader and detective in training for Pavel Baranov

Vinokurov, Jaroslav: Second surveyor.

Zuykov, Viktor: detective corporal, Ufa police